LOSING
Elizabeth

TANYA J. PETERSON

ISBN-10: 1468188283
ISBN-13: 9781468188288 NA
Library of Congress Control Number: 2012900589
CreateSpace, North Charleston, SC

For Hailey and Avery.
May you remain strong in your relationships.

CHAPTER 1

"**E**lizabeth? Lizzie, sweetheart, it's all right."
Elizabeth recognized her mother's voice. She opened her eyes, but the blinding white light assaulted them. She quickly closed them again.

"She's awake; that's a good sign. She'll probably be groggy and confused for a while, but she will come around. She suffered a nasty blow to the head, but nothing that will cause permanent damage. She has three cracked ribs and several deep contusions on her back, sides, and stomach. Her elbow is sprained. Keeping it stable in the sling for at least a week is important. The abrasions on her arm look terrible, but they're not deep. They'll heal quickly. I know she looks bad, but she is okay. I promise."

Elizabeth heard Dr. Gray's voice through a haze. She tried to open her eyes again, but everything was a blur and the lights were just too bright. It was too hard to concentrate. She felt so exhausted.

"I want to keep her here for a couple of days." Dr. Gray continued to talk to Elizabeth's parents. "We need to watch that concussion. The police will also need to talk to Elizabeth as soon as possible. In cases of assault, they need to find out exactly what happened. The sooner they can talk to a victim, the more accurate the description of the event is. That will help them find the attacker."

Assault. Attacker. Elizabeth cringed inwardly at the words. Her stomach jumped in anxiety, but then it hurt. Everything hurt. The police would be talking to her. What could she even say? She felt so confused. She didn't even understand it herself. Here she was in the hospital, and she'd been badly beaten, but she was confused about it. How in the world did she wind up here? How did it get this far? How did it even start? She thought she knew the answer to that. It was just before school started this fall...

CHAPTER 2

Thwack! Elizabeth Carter felt the ball hit the sweet spot of her racket firmly and watched with satisfaction as it sped across the court, just inches above the net. Instinctively she sprang into action, swiftly shuffling to the back center of the tennis court. Gripping her racket loosely in her hand and bouncing lightly on the balls of her feet, Elizabeth anticipated the ball's return to her side of the court. Smack! Here it comes, she thought. She darted forward, ready to swing. Her eyes followed the ball's flight, right into the net on the other side of the court.

"Awesome serve, Lizzie! That had some punch! I felt that one all the way up to my shoulder!" Her best friend, Meg Turner, shouted her support from the other side of the net.

"Aw, Meg! You could have returned it. It wasn't *that* good."

Meg jogged up to the net to talk to Elizabeth. "Yes it was! You don't even realize how good you're getting, Elizabeth. Coach Thompson was watching that serve. I'm telling you, he's got his eye on you for varsity!"

"What were you doing watching Coach Thompson? Meg, he'd be watching you for varsity, too, if you'd concentrate more on the game."

Coach Thompson bellowed from across the row of green and red tennis courts. "I'm not going to consider either of you girls for varsity if you don't get back to practice! You two look like Wilma Flintstone and Betty Rubble, talking across the net like that. Now get back to the game!"

"I'd be glad to be Betty Rubble if he'd be Barney."

"Meg!"

"Well, I would. Talk to you later."

———

The smell of the freshly mowed grass permeated her nose and invigorated her as she jogged lap after lap around the tennis court. Elizabeth loved the way working out always made her feel. With her heart rate elevated and lungs working overtime to supply oxygen to her tired muscles, she felt alive. It was unseasonably cool today in Chesterville Vermont, and the clean air bathed her skin in its crispness and made her feel refreshed despite the long, hard tennis practice.

Meg jogged up beside her and panted, "I envy you. You always look so relaxed when you're running laps. How do you do it?"

"I don't know; it just feels good. You looked good out there once you started paying attention, Meg."

"Thanks! We'll never make the top spots—the seniors will get those—but I wonder if we'll make the varsity team. Juniors are eligible. Maybe we'll earn spots four and five. That wouldn't be bad."

"You know, it might happen. Six out of fourteen girls aren't the best odds, but they're not bad, and you and I are playing pretty good this year, aren't we?"

"Look, Lizzie—Thompson is watching us again. Do you think he's looking to see if we have what it takes, or do you think he's checking me out?"

"I'm sure he's trying to gather up the nerve to ask if you want to go to the football game with him tonight." Elizabeth giggled. "Then maybe you can invite him back to your house. He can meet your parents, then you can show him the Barbies you still have in your room."

"Knock it off! I can dream, can't I? Speaking of tonight, are we going to the game?"

"Of course! The first home football game is always really fun, especially when school hasn't even started yet. Everyone goes."

"We've got to go to Grizzly's afterward! I've been looking forward to the great junior-senior hangout since seventh grade. I can't wait! I wonder what it's really like."

"Hey Meg, most of the football players usually show up there. Maybe Brad will be there. Maybe he'll notice me!"

"Brad? Brad Evans? Oh, now who's dreaming, Lizzie? He's only the hottest senior in the state. Every girl in school has her eye on him—hey, even I would dump Coach Thompson for Brad Evans."

"You can't dump Coach Thompson, Meg. You're not dating him."

"That's beside the point. Anyway, Brad can have any girl he wants. That's not to say he won't notice you, though, especially if you make number four or five on the tennis team. Then you two would have something in common: you'd both be varsity athletes. I don't know, though. Brad Evans is a pretty lofty goal."

"For goodness' sakes, Meg, I'm not trying to marry the guy. I just thought he might notice me, that's all."

"Whatever. See you tonight!"

After practice, Elizabeth jogged all the way home. She felt good. She had a chance to be on the varsity tennis team; she and Meg were going to the football game and to Grizzly's later; and, as Meg said, she and Brad Evans just might have something in common. If he came to Grizzly's tonight, maybe she'd work up the nerve to talk to him. After all, it would be cool to talk to a varsity athlete.

CHAPTER 3

Elizabeth could hear the noise before she, Meg, and their friend Jenny even rounded the corner onto Third Street, or as it was commonly called, Grizzly's street. The noise first reached her ears as a low roar, not unlike the sound heard at lunchtime in the cafeteria of her high school. As they drew closer, sounds began to distinguish themselves. Blaring music escaped through the open windows and door, filling Third Street with a steady, upbeat rhythm. Noises from the kitchen and dining area could also be heard as someone apparently dropped something—probably a rather large stack of now-broken plates, Elizabeth guessed, judging from the crashing sound. Above everything was the sound of her classmates—loud, boisterous, cheerful shouts mixed with surges of laughter. Elizabeth wondered if Grizzly's was always this loud or if the crowd was particularly wound up due to the football team's awesome victory tonight.

As Elizabeth entered Grizzly's, she understood why she could hear the noise from around the corner. The place was packed. A sea of green and gold varsity letter jackets swarmed in front of her. The school colors were splashed everywhere; alternating green and gold tables lined the walls around the perimeter of the entire building, each with green and gold upholstered stools. Pennants, posters, buttons, and bumper stickers heralding the Chesterville Bears adorned the walls. Even the floor was tiled with green, gold, and white. Juniors and seniors from Chesterville High School sat at the tables; mingled on the big, open floor in the center of the "cave," as it was commonly called; and leaned on the order counter at the back of the room.

"Wow! This is incredible!" exclaimed Meg.

Jenny was equally impressed. "This is more colorful than the school! And look at all the people! I bet almost every junior and senior from CHS is here. What do you think, Elizabeth?"

"I think I'm hungry. I smell nachos, and I think I just saw someone walk by with a giant pickle. I love those! It makes sense that they sell them; after all, they're green."

"Lizzie, you make me sick. You can eat and eat, yet look how thin you are. I look at a slice of pizza and gain ten pounds," Meg said.

Elizabeth shook her head and gave her friend a good-natured punch in the arm. "Yeah, right, you twig. Let's go see if we can find a table."

They wove their way through the throng of people and found an unoccupied table in the middle of the seating area. No sooner had they sat down than Elizabeth spotted him. Leaning against the counter, his green and gold letter jacket making his already broad shoulders look huge, Brad was chatting easily with a teammate, smiling and laughing. From time to time he would gesture in the air as if he were throwing a football, catching a football, or tackling somebody.

Elizabeth concentrated on him. *No doubt they're rehashing tonight's game,* she thought. *It's not surprising that so many people admire Brad Evans. He's super hot, for one thing, with his jet-black hair and large, green eyes. People seem to like to be around him because he radiates enthusiasm. Just look at him now. The way he's smiling and gesturing, you'd think he was discussing a Super Bowl he played in, but he's not. He's just excited about his team and their victory tonight. He seems to know so many people. I wonder if he knows who I am.*

"Lizzie, what are you staring at?" asked Meg.

"You guys, look who's over at the counter. It's Brad Evans!"

"Hey, is he still going out with Sarah Wilson? I don't see her here tonight."

"Jeez, Jenny," exclaimed Elizabeth, "where have you been? They broke up this summer. Why do you think I'm even bothering to drool over him?"

"They did? Why?"

"I don't know," answered Meg. "It's kinda strange. I haven't heard much about it—probably because it happened in July. Not many people were around to work the gossip mill. I heard she dumped him, but I also heard that he dumped her."

"I can't imagine why anyone would dump Brad Evans," Elizabeth replied. "He has it all—looks, personality. He's involved in something all school year: football in the fall, basketball in the winter, and track in the spring. Plus, I think he's in some clubs at school. He always seems so nice at school. Like I said, who would dump him?"

"Well, you never know. Maybe Sarah saw something the rest of us don't."

"I doubt it, Jenny," said Meg. "I'm with Lizzie. Who would dump Brad Evans? I bet he dumped her."

"Well, I don't care who dumped who. I'm going up to the counter to get a soda. Maybe I'll just happen to bump into Brad."

Elizabeth felt jittery on her way up to the counter. *I can't believe I'm doing this*, she thought. *He probably doesn't even know who I am. This is so stupid.* Despite the fact that her legs felt as if they were made of rubber and her feet were encased in cement, she kept moving toward the counter. *Oh my gosh. My hands are actually sweaty!* Any appetite that she had earlier was now gone. Her stomach was zinging around inside her more than a tennis ball flew back and forth over the net in a rapid volley. In her mind, she began to panic at the thought that she might actually talk to him.

What am I even going to say to him? Maybe I should mention something from tonight's game. But should I mention a play he was involved in, or would that look like I was watching him? If I just mention the victory, that will seem trite. I don't know much about football, though. I wish I would have watched more Sunday afternoon football with Dad all these years! Oh, well, I'll think of something.

Before she even reached the counter, Elizabeth saw Brad glance her way and excuse himself from his conversation. *Oh, wow! He's coming over here! I hope I can think of something to say*, she worried.

"Hi. Aren't you Elizabeth Carter?"

"Yes." *Oh, that was smooth, Elizabeth*, she thought to herself. *Way to impress him right off the bat.*

"I thought so. You're on the tennis team, aren't you?"

"Yes." *Another witty retort.*

"I'm Brad."

"I know! You're Brad Evans. I'm just surprised that you know who I am." *You're not supposed to admit that, Elizabeth, jeez.*

"Of course I do. I've known about you for some time now, but I'd like to know more. Want to find a nice, quiet table?"

Elizabeth laughed. "A quiet table? In here?"

"Well, how about a noisy table?"

Brad ordered Cokes and led Elizabeth toward a table that two other people had just deserted. She dropped behind him and waved toward Meg and Jenny. "Brad Evans!" she mouthed toward them as she walked behind Brad. Meg flashed her a thumbs-up sign and a huge grin.

When they reached the table, Brad set the Cokes down and pulled out a chair, indicating that Elizabeth should sit down. *Smooth guy*, she thought. *I wonder if Meg and Jenny are watching.*

"Thank you. That was nice."

"Well, I like to do nice things for nice girls. Plus I'm trying to impress you. Did it work?"

"You bet! I'm impressed!"

"Good. You impress me, too. I hear you could earn a varsity slot on this year's tennis team. That's great, considering how many returning seniors are on the team."

"Yeah, I'm sort of worried about that. We've got a lot of good, experienced talent this year. Well, I'm not worried about the fact that we have lots of talent—that will make us a strong team. We're already hoping to take state and we haven't even had a match yet. But I am concerned that I won't make varsity. There are fourteen players on the team, and only six make up the varsity squad."

"From what I hear, it's the other players who have to worry about you."

"I don't know. What I *do* know is that I hate this part of the season. I can't wait until tomorrow; it's the final day of matches against fellow teammates. Coach Thompson will evaluate our playing, look at our win-loss record against each other, and then seed all of us. Then we can stop competing with each other and start working together as a team to be the best tennis team in the state. I really want to be a varsity player this year, but I know that I still have one year ahead of me to do that."

Just then some overzealous dancers bumped their table. Their drinks toppled over, sending ice and sticky Coke scattering over the edge of the table and into their laps. "Hey! Watch it!" Brad roared over the noise of the crowd as he leaped up, furious. "Damn it! Look at us!" He began to vigorously sponge himself off with his napkin.

Elizabeth dabbed at her own lap. "It's okay, Brad. It's just soda. I don't mind. I'm surprised that it took this long for something like this to happen. This place is packed!"

"You're right," he said as he calmed down. "I just was upset for you. I didn't know how you'd feel about having Coke spilled on that amazing outfit. Why don't we get out of here so we can talk more easily? Where would you like to go?"

"Actually, I have to be home by eleven and it's already after ten. I guess we really can't do much, can we?" Elizabeth's heart sank. *Shoot. Stupid curfew. I hope I didn't just make him think that I'm totally lame. He'll probably never talk to me again after tonight.*

"No problem. Can I walk you home? Sorry I can't drive you, but I rode with Mark Higgins tonight so I don't have a car of my own."

"I'd like that."

They stood and headed for the door. Elizabeth left without so much as a glance back at Meg and Jenny.

The cool, quiet night was a refreshing change from the intensity of Grizzly's. Away from the hectic atmosphere, they were able to resume their conversation in peace.

"We were talking about the tennis team before we were so rudely interrupted," he said. "I bet you'll be a two-year varsity player. You've got a lot of potential."

"Hey, how do you know so much about my tennis potential, anyway?"

"Because I'm Brad Evans, that's how."

"Seriously." She gave him a pointed look.

"Because I've been attracted to you for some time. I noticed you last year. You're pretty, you seem intelligent, you're a good athlete—I know because I know some of the people on the team and I've asked them about you. I couldn't do anything before because I was going out with Sarah, but now I'm not, so I'd like to get to know you better. Seriously."

Elizabeth's stomach began to zing around again, but this time in a happy way. She felt as if she could float off into the sky at any minute, but she didn't want to. She wanted to stay right here and talk to Brad, the senior she had admired for over a year. He was good-looking, nice, and friendly, and he was involved in many things and liked by many people. She'd always thought he didn't know she existed, but he just admitted that he'd been admiring her for some time and even asked other people about her. She pinched herself in the leg when he wasn't looking just to make sure she wasn't dreaming. Nothing happened. It was real, then! Brad Evans was really walking her home! Brad was with her, Elizabeth Carter, when he could be back at Grizzly's or anywhere else with anyone he wanted to be with. Wow! She wiggled her toes in her shoes as her stomach did another zing—a really big one.

They walked slowly toward her house. Stars twinkled above them in the night sky. An occasional streetlight lit up a patch of sidewalk for them, but they didn't really need it because the full moon illuminated everything around them. Crickets serenaded them from their hiding places in the lawns, and fallen leaves crunched beneath their feet. Elizabeth barely registered all of this; she was too caught up in the fact that Brad was escorting her home. About halfway to her house, he gently put his hand around hers and her heart did a dance. They chatted easily about tennis, football, and school until they reached Elizabeth's front steps.

"It's been great talking to you tonight, Elizabeth."

"I agree. I'm so glad I came to Grizzly's tonight."

"Me, too. I didn't find out enough about you, though. Could we get together again soon, maybe even tomorrow?"

"I'd love that! I've got tennis practice and my final matches in the morning and afternoon, but after that I'm free."

"Great! Would you mind if I came by the courts to watch you? I've heard that you're good, but I'd like to see you for myself."

"Wow. You'd come see me at practice?"

"You bet. Football practice is in the morning; we have to review the film of tonight's game and run drills. It's over in the afternoon, though. If you don't mind, I'll come to see you when my practice is over."

"I'll watch for you."

"Great. Good night, Elizabeth."

"Good night, Brad."

He turned and walked back down the sidewalk. She watched him go, and then ran inside the house. She knew her mom would still be up, puttering around doing little chores. She couldn't wait to tell her about who she had spent the evening with!

CHAPTER 4

"**T**hanks a lot for ditching us last night." On the courts before practice, Meg ran up behind her best friend and threw her arm around her shoulders.

"Oh, Meg, I couldn't wait to see you today! First, I'm so sorry for leaving like that. I just got so caught up in the moment. Are you mad?"

"Are you kidding? Why would I be mad for that? I would have done the same thing and you know it. But I will be mad if you don't give me all of the details about what happened."

"It was incredible! It—"

Coach Thompson blew his whistle, signaling the beginning of practice. The girls gathered around him in the center of the courts. "I'll tell you about it later," whispered Elizabeth.

"All right, girls, this is it. Today is the day you get your spots on the team. You've been drilling and working and playing matches against each other. Looking at those results, I matched you up for today's final rounds. Each of you will be playing matches against two different people.

I'll look at the scores of your games, the results of your sets, and who won each match. Then I'll let you know your positions for the season. Let's do some warm-ups."

As Elizabeth moved through her warm-up drills, intense concentration on today's matches replaced her thoughts of Brad. Even though she knew that she was only a junior and could still play varsity next year, she desperately wanted to be on the varsity team this year. She'd been dreaming of it ever since she began to play in grade school. She loved tennis. She loved the feel of the racket in her hand—slightly heavy, but not too much so; it felt like a natural extension of her arm. She loved calculating the direction the ball would take as it left her opponent's racket and springing into action as it flew to her side of the court. She loved darting up and down, back and forth across the court, and she loved making her opponent do the same. She loved the exhilarating feel that came from a hard-driven, well-placed shot that her opponent just couldn't return. She enjoyed playing tennis all the time, but especially when she was competing in a match that counted for something, like helping her school's team win a competition. Since varsity players competed in more matches than junior varsity players, she badly wanted to be on the varsity team.

The day flew by as Elizabeth moved through her games. She lost some, but she won more, and she felt that her performance was pretty good overall. She was tired yet elated when Coach Thompson called the group together again. He congratulated the girls, radiating pride at their performance as he claimed that they were sure to take state this year if they all continued to play this well. He sent them off to run laps and cool down while he calculated the scores and seeded the players, assigning them their ranking on the team. Meg hurried toward Elizabeth and matched her stride.

"Lizzie, Lizzie! I've been trying to get your attention. Look who's here!" She gestured toward the north end of the courts where Brad sat on a bench, leaning forward with his elbows on his knees and hands balled under his chin, and staring at the courts.

"Wow! He actually came! He told me he was going to, but I wasn't sure that he would, especially after I told him I had that curfew. Meg, can you believe it? Brad Evans came to watch me, Elizabeth Carter, play tennis! And it's only a practice!" She smiled and waved at him, and her stomach jumped in glee as he waved back. "Oh my gosh! How do I look? Don't tell me. I look awful. My hair always gets matted all over my head when I play. I bet my stupid ponytail looks like a wet weasel, and I'm totally sweating. Oh, no! How long has he been here?"

"Relax, will you? You look fine. He's an athlete; he understands how people look when they work out. Besides, you never look awful. Me on the other hand—well, that's a different issue. Anyway, Brad's been here for a while. He got to see you play, and you looked impressive. I was watching you and Brad between shots."

"Meg!"

"Well, my matches were going fine, and I just had to see what was going on between you two."

"You're unbelievable. Hey! It looks like Coach Thompson is finished. Yes! He's blowing his whistle. Oh, I hope we made it! Good luck, Meg. Let's go."

Coach Thompson began with a pep talk that, although encouraging and motivating, seemed to last for hours. Elizabeth couldn't sit still during the entire speech; she bounced her knees up and down and twirled her racket in her hand. From time to time, she glanced in Brad's direction. He was still watching. She began to grow impatient. She wanted to know if she made varsity and she wanted to run and tell Brad how she did. Finally, Coach Thompson got to the list.

"Playing first for the Chesterville Bears this year will be Holly McIntyre. Second is Jenna Stevens. Third, Tricia Algood. Fourth, Elizabeth Carter. Fifth..."

Elizabeth's stomach was doing flips, and she felt as though she were up in the clouds. She barely repressed a whoop of glee. *Fourth! I made the fourth spot! I'm a varsity player! Meg was right. The top spots went to seniors, but I'm on the varsity! There are seniors behind me. I get to compete at the varsity level!*

Elizabeth focused her attention again just in time to hear Coach Thompson announce Meg's name. "Now for our junior varsity players. Meg Turner will be heading the JV team at slot number seven..."

Elizabeth's excitement dwindled slightly. *Oh, poor Meg! She didn't make the varsity team. She missed it by one position. I wonder how she feels.*

As soon as Coach Thompson dismissed the team for the day, Elizabeth turned to Meg. "Meg, I'm so sorry. You were so close. But you are number seven, the leader of the JV team. That's great! And you'll be first to move up to varsity if anything happens this year."

"Yeah, I know." Her voice wasn't quite as peppy as usual. "But hey, I am so happy for you, Lizzie. I knew you'd make it! You can fill me in about life at the top."

"I'm not exactly at the top. I'm only three spots ahead of you. I'd say we're pretty close."

"Actually, want to know my theory? I think Coach Thompson just didn't want me to be on varsity because it could make me too tired. Then I wouldn't have much energy for him after practice."

"Meg!"

They walked slowly to the gate as they talked. Brad sauntered down from his place on the bench. "You looked great out there, Elizabeth! I bet you made varsity! Were you planning on coming to tell me, or do I have to read about it in the school paper?"

"Brad, I'm glad you came! I made varsity; I'm number four! Meg is number seven."

"Oh, hi, Meg," he added belatedly. "Number four. That's close to varsity. Elizabeth, you made varsity! That's great! Can we go out to celebrate?"

Meg answered first. "Well, Elizabeth and I had plans, but I guess I'll let her off the hook just this once."

Elizabeth turned toward her best friend. "Oh, Meg, do you mind? I really feel guilty just abandoning you and our plans." Her stomach felt all twisted up. *This is how a tennis ball must feel, flying back and forth across the net.* She was so excited and happy about being on the varsity team and having Brad there to watch and ask her out on a date, but she also felt really bad for Meg. Meg didn't make varsity and Elizabeth could tell she was feeling low, and to top it off, her best friend was considering abandoning her just to go out with a guy. *But he's such a great guy.*

"I'm actually wiped out from today," replied Meg. "I wouldn't mind not doing anything tonight, Lizzie. Call me tomorrow, though."

"You got it! Meg, you're the best." Elizabeth turned to Brad. "Well, how should we celebrate?"

"How about a movie and pizza afterward? Are you going home to shower first?"

"Definitely."

"Why don't I pick you up at your house in about two hours?"

"Great! See you then."

———

Elizabeth burst through her front door so quickly that she didn't even stop to put her tennis racket down. She ran through the house shouting, "Mom! Mom! Guess what? I did it! I made varsity! And Brad Evans asked me out tonight! Life is great!"

Her mother came running down the stairs. "Oh, Lizzie! Varsity! I knew you would do it. What a great coach you have; he knows talent when he sees it. What's this about Brad? He really came to your practice? Wow. He seems like a great guy. He must be really interested in you."

"Oh, I hope so. Come help me decide what to wear."

When Brad rang the doorbell two hours later, Elizabeth came down the steps looking refreshed and radiant. Gone were the ponytail and tennis shorts—her chestnut hair now hung down just past her shoulders. She had it tucked back behind her ears, which accentuated the soft curls at the ends. She wore an olive green ankle-length skirt printed with little leaves of pink, yellow, and light olive. Her olive-colored shirt complemented her brown eyes and her summer tan earned by long hours on the tennis court.

"Wow! You look great. Are you sure you're the same Elizabeth Carter I saw just two hours ago?"

"Believe it or not, it's me. You don't look so bad yourself." His straight hair was combed down on his forehead but stopped well above his eyebrows, giving him a very innocent appearance. He looked very fit and handsome in khakis and a deep purple long-sleeved crew shirt.

Elizabeth was glad she had chosen the outfit she did. It complemented Brad's well—not too casual, but not too dressy, either.

"Brad, this is my mom."

Brad extended his hand. "It's nice to meet you, Mrs. Carter."

"Likewise. Would you like to come in? We have refreshments in the kitchen."

"I'm sorry, but Elizabeth and I had better get going if we're going to catch the movie."

"Of course; maybe another time. Elizabeth, remember your eleven thirty curfew, and have a fun time."

"I will. Bye!" Once they were out the door, Elizabeth turned to Brad. "Wow, she must approve of you. She extended my curfew! Be glad my dad was working late tonight. I think she was disappointed, though, that we didn't stay for just a little while."

"Well, do you want to hang around your house with your mom, or do you want to go out?" He sounded just a little irritated.

"Of course I want to go out. So let's go!"

Brad's mood improved considerably once they drove off. Elizabeth figured that he had been nervous about meeting her mother. *I guess I don't blame him,* she thought. *It would be hard to be a guy, having to ask a girl out on a date, pick her up, and meet her parents.*

As planned, they first went to a movie starring Johnny Depp, an actor they both liked. After the show, they went to a local pizza place to eat and continue to get to know each other.

Brad began by asking about her family. "So, you said your dad was working late. If he had been home, would they both have met me together?"

"Yeah. They're like that. Why?"

"Just wondering. They must get along, then."

"I guess. I've never thought about it, actually. They don't fight, if that's what you mean."

He hesitated before he spoke. "I haven't really told anybody this, and I wasn't going to say anything to you. I promised myself I wouldn't tell anybody, but I feel comfortable around you. My parents are getting a divorce. My dad moved out this summer. My brother went with him, but I'm staying with my mom. I guess Kyle—that's my brother; he's twelve—always got along better with my dad than I did. That's why he moved out with him. My dad bought me the used car I have and gives me an allowance, and he thinks that's enough to fulfill his fatherly duties with me."

"Oh, no. Brad, I'm so sorry. I can't imagine what it would be like if my dad moved out and my parents got divorced. It must be pretty awful."

"It is," he said quietly. "But, hey, I don't want to ruin our first date. Let's talk about something more upbeat. I've been wondering what you plan to do after high school."

"Brad, do you want to talk about your dad a little more first? I'm a great listener."

"No. I want to hear about your plans."

Elizabeth respected that the subject was closed. "Well, I want to be an engineer. I love computers, math, and science, and I love building things and solving problems. You should have seen what I could do with Tinker Toys when I was little!"

"Wow, an engineer. There aren't a lot of female engineers, are there?"

"Not really. It's a pretty male-dominated field, but I figure that might work to my advantage. I could offer a fresh, new perspective to companies needing engineers."

"Do you think it'll be tough to get into a good college?"

"I don't know. I'll be taking college prep and advanced placement classes at school this year and next, which will help. And I'm involved in lots of things— tennis, the computer club, the environmental club, ice-skating in the winter, and hopefully I'll be in school plays. I've heard that colleges look for people who participate in activities. They like 'well-rounded' people, or something like that."

"That's true. I was in some clubs last year. I wasn't planning on joining any this year, but the computer club and the environmental club are starting to look pretty good!" He winked at her, and she grinned at him before sinking her teeth into a slice of pepperoni pizza. Brad continued, "I'd really like to get into a big college on a football scholarship. There were some scouts watching me at the end of last season, and Coach told me some have been asking about me this year. They'll start coming to games soon. I'm excited, but nervous."

"I think you'll have colleges from all over the country begging to have you come play for them."

"I hope so. I really need a good scholarship now. With my parents divorced, paying for college could be difficult. My dad has Kyle to raise, and my mom doesn't make a lot of money. The child support money my dad will pay won't be enough to put me through college, and my allowance helps but isn't exactly designed to cover school costs. I really want to go to college and play football."

"I know the feeling. College is really important to me, too. More than anything, I want to be an engineer."

Elizabeth and Brad spent some more time talking. They shared stories about their families, school experiences, and other plans for the future. By the time he drove her home, Elizabeth felt that they had known each other forever. She liked him a lot.

That night, just before she crawled into bed, she felt so many good things inside her about what had happened today that she couldn't contain them any longer. She did a dance all around her room, the way she used to do when she was younger whenever something good happened to her. She even indulged in a bounce on her bed before flopping down and drifting off to sleep with a smile on her face.

CHAPTER 5

"**P**acked" didn't even begin to describe the Chesterville High gymnasium. Jammed, bustling, and hectic were words that popped into Meg's mind as she pushed her way to the "S-Z" table. It was 7:45 in the morning on the first day of school, and students mingled around the gym. They were supposed to be finding their appropriate table—set up in alphabetical order according to their last names—to obtain their class schedules, locker assignments, and lunch times. The students were doing just that, but they were also mingling about, enthusiastically greeting people they hadn't seen much over the summer, talking with friends they had seen at Friday's football game, discussing things that had happened that weekend or over the summer, and comparing schedules. Meg found it very chaotic, and she loved it. There was something about the morning of the first day of school that excited her. She loved seeing all the people milling about, reacting to their schedules, talking to each other. Spirits were always high on the first day of school.

She worked her way through her line, got her information, and talked to what seemed like a hundred people before she finally found the person she was looking for. "Elizabeth!" She shouted over the noise. She had to shout three more times before Elizabeth heard her. "Hey, stranger! Let's see your schedule. What lunch do you have? How was your date with Brad? Sorry I missed your call yesterday and couldn't even text. I ended up going out of town with my family and it was one of their 'no technology' days. You didn't answer my question—how was your date with Brad?"

Elizabeth laughed and pulled her friend out of the gym and into the hallway where people were walking around, finding their classrooms and their lockers. "It's hard to believe, but you are even more hyper on the first day of school than you normally are! First things first: what lunch do you have, and how many classes do we have together?"

Meg compared her schedule with Elizabeth's and found that they had sixth period English together. She was also delighted to learn that they had the same lunch. They stood outside the gym waiting for Jenny and comparing schedules with other friends who passed by. Between conversations with other students, Meg listened to Elizabeth's "Brad details."

"Oh, Elizabeth! He sounds perfect! You are *sooooooo* lucky!" Suddenly, she poked Elizabeth. "Look who's coming! It's Brad!" He approached and sidled up very close to Elizabeth. Meg raised her eyebrows at her, indicating that she noticed.

Brad nodded at her, and then spoke to Elizabeth. "Hey. I've been looking all over for you; I figured you would be in the gym. I'm surprised to see you out here."

Meg wasn't sure, but she thought Brad sounded a little angry. *He's probably just stressed from all of this first day stuff. I like the first day, but a lot of people don't. Lizzie doesn't seem to notice anything. I'm sure it's nothing.*

"Great! I've got that lunch, too," Brad was telling Elizabeth. "Come on. Let's go find our classes before first period begins."

Meg joined their conversation. "You go ahead, Lizzie. I'm going to wait for Jenny. I'll see you at lunch."

She frowned as she watched Elizabeth and Brad go off together. She was genuinely happy for her best friend and wanted her to get together with the guy she'd been dreaming about, but something about him was bothering her. She forgot her concern, however, when she saw Jenny walking out of the gym, schedule in hand. "Hey, Jen, over here!" She waved and moved toward Jenny.

The girls compared schedules and found that they had trigonometry, chemistry, and lunch together. "Lizzie has lunch with us, too," Meg said.

"Great! Speaking of her, where is she?"

"She went with Brad to find their lockers and rooms. Can you believe it? She's walking the halls with a senior— and not just any senior, mind you. And guess what? He walked her home Friday night after they left Grizzly's, came to our tennis practice on Saturday, and they went out Saturday night. I don't know if anything happened on Sunday because I wasn't around. Now they're already together this morning."

"Wow. They're moving fast."

"Totally. Lizzie seems thrilled."

"*Oooh*, Meg. What's with that tone? You're not jealous, are you?"

"Of course not! I'm excited for her. It's just that I've been around him twice now, and something about him bothers me. He's great to Elizabeth, so that's not it. I don't know..."

Jenny couldn't help but laugh. "Did he fall all over you, or just Elizabeth?"

"I'm not even sure if he realized I was standing there either time, actually. Why?"

Jenny chuckled again. "Oh, Meg. You're so used to people giving you lots of attention that you probably don't know how to handle this. No, don't look at me like that—I know you're not jealous. That's not what I'm saying. I just mean that maybe you were thrown off a little because he didn't pay attention to you. Am I right?"

At that, Meg couldn't help but grin. "I guess you're right. Oh my gosh! It's almost eight thirty. We'd better get to math. Come on, let's hurry!"

Meg and Jenny ran down the halls of CHS and into their first classroom just in time. After that, Meg didn't have time to give much thought to anything other than her classes as the day rushed by. Before she knew it, she was in the cafeteria joining Elizabeth and Jenny for lunch.

"Hey, girlfriends! How's your first day going?" Meg asked as they all sat down at an empty table.

Jenny answered first. "Crazy. I've actually got homework already! And an essay for American History class."

"You must have Heidenrich for history, then. I've got the same assignment," Elizabeth commented.

"You think that's bad," Meg chimed in, "I've got a test on Thursday in biology!"

"Biology?" Jenny asked. "But you're in my chemistry class. Why do you have two science classes?"

"Because my parents thought that it would be a good idea to take all the science classes this school has to offer.

It will help me get into a good college, which will help me get into a good med school. That's important, you know, if I'm going to be a specialist."

"What kind of a specialist?" asked Jenny.

"My parents and I aren't sure yet, but I have to start preparing anyway."

Jenny was puzzled. "Your parents—"

Elizabeth cut her off. "Speaking of your parents, Meg, how did they take the news that you're not on the varsity team this year?" she asked, concerned.

"Well, they didn't kick me out of the house or anything. They said it was no big deal, that they were proud that I'm the leader of the JV team, but I could tell that they were disappointed. I know they wanted me to be a two-year varsity player."

Elizabeth was quick to reassure Meg, who seemed a little down. "Bummer. I know them, though, Meg, and when they say they're proud of you, they really do mean it. And they should be proud—you earned a great position on the team."

"Look, Jenny, someone from the upper ranks on the tennis team is trying to encourage one of the little people!" Meg grinned and laughed good-naturedly.

Just then, Brad plopped down by Elizabeth. "Hi! What a crazy morning! I'd love to hear how your first day is going, Elizabeth. Want to come over to my table and share horror stories about our classes?" He gestured toward a table that was empty except for one tray—his. "I've reserved a table for two."

"Who else but Brad Evans could pull that off?" Jenny exclaimed, impressed.

"You bet," Brad said with a wink toward Elizabeth. "Should we go?"

Elizabeth hesitated and looked at her friends. "Well, I've already got my stuff set up here, but..."

"Are you nuts, Lizzie? It's a lunch tray, not a seven-course meal. Get up and go!"

Brad didn't respond, but Elizabeth did. "Thanks. I'll catch you guys later. Oh, I guess I'll see you next period, Meg. Bye, guys!" With that, she went off with Brad.

After they had gone, Meg turned to Jenny. "See what I mean? He's awesome, but there's something...I don't know. He really is cute, though, isn't he? And look how he is with Elizabeth. He gives her all of his attention and treats her like she's the only person in the world worth being with." With that statement, Meg brightened considerably. "That's it! I was worried over nothing this morning. To Brad, Lizzie is the only person in the world right now. That's why he really doesn't give me—or you, did you notice?—the time of day. He's interested only in Lizzie! Oh, she's lucky!"

"I think you're right, Meg. There's nothing to be bothered about. That's so cool! I wish a guy would treat me that way."

"Well, Jenny, I'm not bothered about Lizzie, but I am bothered about biology. That test is going to be a monster, and it's only the beginning of the school year!"

CHAPTER 6

After the first day of school, Elizabeth's routine was established. Her mornings went quickly as she moved from class to class. She was happy to have her favorite classes, Trigonometry II and physics, early in the day. Those classes were challenging and exciting and helped make time fly by. Even so, mornings never moved quite fast enough. The highlight of Elizabeth's school day was eating lunch with Brad at "their" table. She missed eating with Meg and Jenny, but Brad had convinced her on day one that lunch should be their special time, as they had no classes together. Besides, she saw Meg every day after lunch in English class and again at tennis practice, so she had plenty of chances to talk to her.

The rest of Elizabeth's time had fallen into a pattern, too. She had three more classes after lunch and then it was off to tennis practice. Brad's football practice ended at approximately the same time as tennis ended, so he always came by to take her home. They usually took more time than was needed to get from the tennis courts to her house. Then it was supper, homework (she usually had tons), texting Brad and Meg while studying, a chat on the phone with Brad, and then bedtime to rest up for another busy day. Her crazy, wonderful schedule made the first weeks of school whiz along.

Word had spread like wildfire throughout the school that Elizabeth Carter and Brad Evans were an item. Elizabeth was amused that the entire school had begun to view them as a couple by the end of the second day of school, but she also found it exciting. Last year Sarah Wilson was the envy of every girl in school. *Now it's my turn,* Elizabeth thought happily as she waited for Brad at their lunch table. *Hey, I wonder what Sarah is up to this year. I've seen her around, but I haven't really heard anything about her.*

Actually, Elizabeth had seen her several times recently; she often noticed Sarah standing a short distance from her locker. It was almost as if she were waiting for a chance to approach her, but each time she turned and walked away. Elizabeth always dismissed Sarah's actions. *She's probably just a bit jealous that Brad has another girlfriend. I still don't know what happened between them, but the fact that he's dating someone else now is probably hard for her to take,* she mused as she waited for Brad at their usual place in the cafeteria. She had been texting Meg while she waited.

"What's a beautiful girl like you doing sitting alone in a place like this?" A deep voice interrupted her thoughts.

"Just waiting for a handsome prince to come by and rescue me. Want to interview for the position?" She threw her phone in her bag and grinned up at her boyfriend.

"Consider the job taken," he replied.

"Speaking of sitting alone, Meg was just saying that we should join her and Jenny at lunch sometimes. What do you think?" When he just stared at her, she continued. "Well, I don't mean every day, but once in a while it'd be okay. Some of your friends sit at that table, too, so I think it would be fun. Brad?"

He stared at her in stony silence, and she shifted uneasily. She hadn't realized until now just how hard and uncomfortable the plastic cafeteria chairs were. Finally he spoke. "I thought you liked eating lunch with me," he said coolly.

"I do! It's the best part of the school day. It's just that..."

"It's just that what?"

"I thought we would enjoy having lunch together with our friends sometimes, that's all."

"I can't believe you would rather spend your short lunch period with those bimbos than with me."

"Brad, I wanted you to come along, too. Look, like I said, some of your friends eat over there. Hey! What do you mean 'bimbos'?"

"You know exactly what I mean, Elizabeth. Meg is just about the flightiest person I've ever met. She has nothing interesting to say, and she needs to be sedated. Don't you find her, uh, enthusiasm, a bit much? And that Jenny—she's just as bad. She has no personality of her own; she just follows Meg around. Shows how stupid she is, too. I mean, if she's going to follow someone around, why Meg?"

Elizabeth couldn't believe what she was hearing. Her boyfriend was attacking her two best friends! "Look, Brad, you're way out of line. Meg—"

Brad cut her off. "Meg what? What redeeming qualities could she possibly have?"

"She's fun to be around and she's a good friend. I can talk to her about anything." Elizabeth felt a strong desire to defend her friend. "She—"

"You've just described a dog, Elizabeth. Dogs are great fun, and you can talk to them about anything, too, because they aren't intelligent enough to understand what you tell them. Come on, you can't tell me that you've never been annoyed that Meg is so hyper and doesn't talk about anything intelligent." Elizabeth didn't answer, which gave Brad the opportunity to continue. "Elizabeth, look, you've really got it together. You're very smart, you're athletic, you're witty, you've got a great boyfriend"—at that, Brad wiggled his eyebrows at her and she couldn't help but smile—"you've got a great goal for the future. Does Meg even have a concept of the future?"

"As a matter of fact, she's planning to become a doctor." She didn't add that that was only because her parents wanted her to and that Meg really had no idea what she wanted for herself.

"Anyone can say that; she's probably just trying to impress you. You're great, Elizabeth. I don't think Meg is very good for you. People think she's flighty, and they will have the same opinion of you if you keep hanging around with her."

Elizabeth felt numb. Her initial anger at Brad had cooled, and now she wasn't quite sure what to feel. On the one hand, he had just given her some very nice compliments that made her feel very good. But on the other hand, he had just insulted her best friend, someone with whom she'd shared ups and downs and fun times for years. She didn't even know how to respond to anything he had said. She merely rested her elbow on the table, chin in hand, tucked a strand of hair behind her ear, and looked down at her untouched food. After a minute or two of silence, Brad spoke again.

"I've upset you. I really didn't mean to. I really enjoy our lunches together and I didn't want this to happen. But it's true—you're awesome, but Meg is...well, she's not. She's annoying. I hate to see you get categorized with her. I like you a lot, Elizabeth. I'm happy with you. In fact, I'm happier now than I have been in a long time. Please don't be upset with me. I was only trying to compliment you and make you see that you don't need Meg and Jenny."

Finally, Elizabeth found her voice. "Brad, the nice things you said about me really mean a lot to me. Those things made me feel very good, but—"

"No 'but,' okay? Let's just leave it at that. Lunch is about over and sixth period is about to begin. Let's go off feeling good. I'll see you after tennis practice?"

Elizabeth thought that his last statement was more of a question, as if he were unsure that she would want to see him later. She looked up to find him staring at her with his big green eyes. His eyebrows were raised ever so slightly, and his lips held just a hint of a tiny smile. He looked innocent and unsure, and any negative feelings that she had for him instantly vanished. "Of course, silly," she replied with a smile. "See you then."

Brad looked so genuinely relieved that she wasn't mad at him that she felt bad for her earlier anger. She reached out to squeeze his hand before walking away, but he surprised her by leaning over and kissing her on the cheek.

He took her hand in his and said, "Come on. I want to walk you to class."

Elizabeth was oblivious to everyone around her as they made their way to her English class. *Wow! Brad kissed me in the middle of the cafeteria! I'll never wash this cheek again!* The thought reminded her of scenes in old TV shows that she had seen, and she laughed aloud at the corniness of it. Brad gave her a quizzical look, and she shrugged. "What can I say? You make me happy."

He gave her another quick peck on the cheek before disappearing back down the hallway toward his own class. Elizabeth felt herself smiling broadly. Her high spirits vanished, however, the moment she saw Meg waiting for her outside the classroom.

"Hey, Lizzie!" Meg came bounding toward her, dropping her books on the way. Unfazed, she picked them up and chattered away. "I was hoping you and Brad would come join us today at lunch. That's okay, though. There's always tomorrow. It looked like you two were having a pretty intense conversation. What were you talking about? Wait until you hear what I heard about Jane Benson. You won't believe it! Only two and a half more hours until tennis practice. I can't wait to see Coach Thompson. Yesterday as I was leaving he told me I was looking good but my serve needed some work. He wants to work with me personally today! I think he's just using that as an excuse to be close to me. What do you think?"

Meg had said all of this before they even reached their desks and sat down. *Brad does have a point*, thought Elizabeth. *Meg is a bit hyper, and she does tend to discuss some shallow things. Wait! What am I thinking? I've always enjoyed her before. But maybe I'm changing.*

Elizabeth's annoyance at herself and at the entire situation caused her to snap at Meg. "Don't be ridiculous, Meg! He's the coach for goodness' sakes. He has to work with members of the team to help them improve. If he didn't, we wouldn't be ranked number one in the state right now, would we? Jeez, Meg." She saw the shocked and hurt expression on her friend's face and instantly regretted her remarks. Thankfully, the bell rang and the teacher started class immediately. They had no opportunity to talk again, and Elizabeth pretended to be so busy she couldn't even look at Meg. When class ended, she took a long time packing up her things. When she finally looked up and started out the door, Meg had already left. Elizabeth was worried that she had really hurt Meg's feelings, but she also was still slightly annoyed at Meg's ramblings before class. *One thing's for certain: I sure am dreading tennis practice.*

———

"So you were telling me that Meg was weird today at practice?" Brad and Elizabeth were involved in their nightly phone conversation. They continued the conversation they had begun when he drove her home from tennis.

"Yeah. I don't know; maybe it was just me. I mean, she was nice and all, but different. She was cordial, but not nearly as talkative or as bouncy as she usually is. She hasn't texted me tonight, either, and she hasn't even logged onto Facebook. I think I really hurt her feelings today in class."

"Well, honestly now, was it really that bad to be withdrawn from Meg?" When the line was silent, he asked again. "Liz? Was it that bad?"

"I guess that's my problem, Brad. No, it wasn't that bad; it was even kind of nice. I could be more serious and concentrate harder on the game. I got much more out of practice than usual, which is especially important now. We'll have very intense practices this week and a big match on Saturday."

"Really?" Elizabeth knew Brad was not happy. Even though she couldn't see his expression, she could hear the tension in his voice. "Tennis takes up so much of your time. I was hoping we could go out on Thursday night and Saturday since our football game is out of town on Friday. I won't be able to see you at all for lunch on Friday, so I wanted to make up for that. But I guess you won't be able to."

Elizabeth ignored the bitter tone she heard in his last statement. She was happy that he was upset that they couldn't spend much time together. "I hate it, too, Brad," she stated regretfully, "but this really is an important week. We're up against some of the top teams in our conference on Saturday; playing well will help us get to state. And anyway, maybe we can go out for a short time after practice on Thursday. I don't think my parents will mind if I go out on a school night one time. And the match will be over by four or five on Saturday. Even if we don't have the afternoon, we'll have all evening to do something."

"That's true, I guess," he relented, "but I wish we had more time together."

"Me, too. Hey! I almost forgot to tell you—you'll be out of town with the football team on Friday, so guess what I'm doing after school? I'm auditioning for the fall play *Great Expectations*! I signed up this morning. I'm excited, but nervous, too. What do you think?"

"What do I think? I think it's stupid!" He practically shouted into the receiver.

His reaction stunned her. After a pause, she managed to ask, "Why?" When he didn't say anything, she continued. "Don't you think I'm suited for it? I know that engineering and acting don't really go together, but engineers need to have fun, too. Plus, having lots of different activities will look great on my college applications. I've always wanted to try a play. I was hoping you'd support me."

"I don't want you to be in a play, Elizabeth. We already don't have enough time together. Now you want to do something else that will take away from us?"

"Brad, that's sweet. I don't want to take time away from us, but I do want to try the play. When you think about it, it really won't change the time we have together. If I make the play, I'll only have a few weeks where I have tennis practice after school and play rehearsal in the evenings. After that it won't be so bad. Besides, that's only if I make it. Who knows? I'm probably the world's worst actress."

"True."

"Thanks a lot, Brad."

"Well, I'm just being realistic. You really have no acting experience, so you might not be cut out for the play."

"I won't know unless I try, though. Now cheer up, Brad. You're still the most important thing in my life."

"Right," he grunted.

"Brad, why are you so crabby today?"

He was silent for a moment, and then snapped, "Because my own father doesn't want me around. My mom will be out of town on business in two weeks, and she wanted me to stay with my dad and Kyle. I kinda wanted that, too, since I haven't seen them in a while, but my dad said no. His apartment is too small or something. First he and Kyle want nothing to do with me, and now it seems that you're abandoning me, too. You'd rather spend time with Meg and the tennis team and now there's the play..." Brad trailed off.

"Oh, Brad, that's not true at all. I can't speak for your dad, but I know that I am crazy about you and want to spend as much time as I can with you. I think you're amazing. I really do."

"Liz, you don't know how much it means to me to hear you say that. Thanks. And you know what? I think you're great, too. I'm glad we're together."

They talked for another half hour. Long after they hung up, Elizabeth could still hear Brad's voice telling her that he was glad they were together. Their arguments today seemed insignificant compared to that.

Just lover's quarrels, she thought, then giggled. Her stomach did a leap at the thought of them being true lovers, and she drifted off to sleep thinking not of Meg, not of tennis, not of her dream to be an engineer, not of the upcoming auditions, but of Brad Evans.

CHAPTER 7

"**E**xcellent muffins, Mom! I think I'll have another one." Elizabeth sat in the kitchen with her mother early Tuesday morning.

"Okay, that's the third compliment you've given me this morning, and it's not even eight o'clock. And while it's certainly nice to hear you say such wonderful things, I can't help but think you're up to something. Out with it—what is it?"

"What?"

"Elizabeth." Her mother's tone was firm, but she was smiling.

"Well, I guess I was just wondering something. I know how you and Dad feel about my going out on school nights, but I was hoping that maybe just this once it would be okay if I went out with Brad on Thursday night." When her mom didn't say anything, she rushed on. "Like I've been telling you, he's really awesome, and he said he's going to miss me on Friday since the football team plays out of town, so he'd like to do something with me Thursday. So what do you think? Can I? Please?" She said all of this almost in one breath, and her mom laughed.

Neither of them had noticed her father leaning against the kitchen doorway. They both jumped when he answered Elizabeth. "I'm glad you know how we feel. We don't think school nights are a good time to be out and about. But I'll tell you what—why don't you invite Brad over here for the evening? We'll all have dinner, and then you and he could spend a couple of hours in the family room. How does that sound?"

"It sounds great! I just think it would be cool to spend time with him Thursday evening. We don't actually have to go anywhere. Thanks, Dad! Now I've gotta run. I've got a test first period, and I don't want to be late. Trig II, you know. I hope I do well. Bye!" With a wave to her parents, she ran out the door.

Elizabeth walked to school in record time, in a hurry to meet Brad. She sent him a text asking him to meet her before class because she wanted to tell him in person, not via cell phone, that he could come over on Thursday. As she left the bright morning sunshine for the darker halls of CHS, she paused for a moment to let her eyes adjust. Immediately, she saw a short figure bouncing toward her. As usual, Meg shouted a greeting before she even reached her.

"Hey, Lizzie! Having a better day? Jeez, what had your shorts in a knot yesterday? Are you and Brad going to join us for lunch today?"

Elizabeth found herself annoyed with Meg. She was impatient to find Brad, and now she had to stop and chat with Meg. *And she is so long-winded. Now I probably won't have time to meet Brad, which means I won't see him until lunch. Why does Meg always have to find me before school anyway?* She just couldn't suppress a sigh as she greeted Meg. "Good morning, Meg."

"Wow, you sure don't sound like the normal Elizabeth. What's up?"

"Look, Meg, I've gotta run. I really need to find Brad before school starts. I'll catch you later, though." Without waiting for her reply, Elizabeth brushed past her and turned down the hallway that led to her locker. She moved away so quickly that she didn't see the hurt look on her best friend's face.

As she worked her way toward her locker, she noticed that she had a stomachache. *Boy, I was really awful to Meg. I should have talked to her for a little bit, but I just couldn't. I can't wait to tell Brad the good news about Thursday. Anyway, Meg's the one who kept encouraging me to go off with Brad, so I'm sure she doesn't mind.* She tried to convince herself that things were okay with Meg, but she was unable to make the hard knot in her stomach disappear. Before she knew it, she was at her locker and Brad was waiting for her.

"Well, good morning to you. Glad you could make it on time."

She thought that he was joking, but she couldn't quite tell. "Hi, Brad," she said weakly.

"Hey, are you all right? What's the matter?" He touched her shoulder and pulled her close, sending little shocks all through her body and completely obliterating her stomachache.

"Nothing, now." She smiled up at him. "I was so excited to get to school today. I've got good news! I couldn't wait to see you before classes began, but then Meg stopped me, and I was pretty rude to her. I didn't want to talk to her. I wanted to find you. I guess that made me feel pretty guilty."

"It shouldn't. Meg is a pain, Elizabeth. You even said yourself that it was nice at tennis practice when you didn't have anything to do with her. You just need to come to terms with the fact that you two have grown apart. You have matured and she hasn't."

"Maybe you're right, but I feel kinda funny about it."

"That will go away sooner than you think. I think you should avoid her from now on. If you continue to talk to her, you'll just string her along. It's not fair to pretend to be nice when your friendship is really over."

"You're probably right. Besides, lately when I talk to her I just end up feeling awful."

"I think I should warn you about something, though. Meg isn't going to be real nice anymore. She'll probably try to hurt you by saying things to break us up. Elizabeth..." He paused, put both hands on her shoulders, and looked her intensely in the eyes. "Please, please, don't let that happen. I'm really crazy about you, and I don't want anything to come between us. Please don't let her attempts to break us up work." His voice was low, and he sounded very solemn and sincere.

Elizabeth felt weak. She was glad he had a firm grip on her shoulders or she would have fallen down right there in the hall. Her heart was racing, and she could barely find her voice. "Oh, Brad," she whispered. "I don't want anyone or anything to come between us, either. I promise I won't let Meg destroy what we have."

Brad grinned from ear to ear, and Elizabeth thought he looked like a little boy who had just received a puppy for Christmas. He gave her shoulders a squeeze then dropped his arms. "Now," he began cheerfully, "what's that good news you wanted to tell me?"

"Oh, it's great! Usually I can't do anything on school nights, but my parents said we could get together on Thursday evening! I can't go out, but they said I could have you over. We'll have supper with them, and then you and I can spend a couple of hours in the family room doing whatever. Maybe we could rent a movie, or we've got tons of games and stuff. Isn't it great?"

"I guess." He sounded less than enthused.

"What's wrong?"

"It's just that I had planned on going to a movie. Can't you talk them into that?"

"No way. I know my parents."

A deep scowl encompassed his entire face. "Jeez. It's going to be like we're back in sixth grade. That's really annoying, Elizabeth."

"Brad, I'm sorry, but it's just the way it is." Her voice quivered ever so slightly.

"Well, it's stupid. How can you stand your parents? Do they always control you this way?" Elizabeth didn't respond but instead looked down at the floor. When she looked up at Brad again, her eyes were brimming with tears. She didn't trust herself to speak, so she remained silent.

After a pause, Brad spoke again. "Oh, Liz, I'm sorry. I'm not really mad at you. Please don't cry. I think your parents are lame for not trusting you enough to go to a movie on a school night, that's all. Look, just this once we'll spend the evening at your house. I'm glad that we'll be together. You are great to be around, and I'm sure we'll have a good time."

"Thanks, Brad. I'm really sorry we can't go out. Thanks for agreeing to come over." She was so wrapped up in her conversation with Brad that she hadn't noticed that the halls were empty. Suddenly, she glanced around with a start. "Oh, no! Brad, what time is it?"

"About eight forty. Classes started ten minutes ago. Didn't you hear the bell?"

"No, I wasn't paying attention. Oh my gosh! My trig test! Brad, I have to go. I'll see you at lunch."

Elizabeth bolted down the hallway and dashed into her seat in the trig room. To her dismay, the class had already started the test. She groaned inwardly when her teacher, Mr. Charlton, summoned her to his desk. *He looks even grouchier than usual*, she thought, her heart sinking. She felt dizzy as she approached his desk. She folded her hands together and cracked her knuckles as she addressed him. "Mr. Charlton, I—"

"Stop cracking those knuckles, Miss Carter. The rest of the class is trying to take a test, in case you haven't noticed." He managed to snap at her even though he spoke in hushed tones. "Do you have a pass?"

"No, I don't. I'm sorry. I was at my locker and didn't realize what time it was. It will never happen again. This grade is important to me, Mr. Charlton. Please, may I take the test?"

"Apparently it's not too important, or you would have kept better track of the time." Looking up at her from his desk, he softened his tone. "I'm sorry, Elizabeth. You are a good student, but I cannot let you take this test. As a junior, you should understand school policy. If you come late to class without a pass, you may not complete any work given during that class period. It is considered an unexcused absence."

"I understand," she managed to squeak out. She shuffled back to her seat and sat down. *Don't cry in class. Don't cry in class.* She repeated this phrase to herself until she felt in control of her emotions. *What a lousy day. First, I find that I've grown apart from my best friend. Then Brad was irritated about having to spend Thursday evening at my house. Now I've missed the trig test. I'll get a zero, and that could really hurt my grade. Why did it have to be a math test? Of all my classes, math and science are then most important.*

She continued to think about her morning. *Well, at least it's clear that Brad cares about me. He actually told me that he's crazy about me!* She sat up a bit straighter in her chair at that thought, but as soon as she looked around at her classmates feverishly working on their tests, she felt bad again. Finally, she decided to write Brad a note, since he seemed to be the only positive thing in her life right now.

Her day didn't improve after first period. Still upset by the morning's events, she found it difficult to concentrate in physics. She only half listened to the teacher's explanation of a new concept, and she didn't really focus on the assigned problems once it came time to work in class; consequently, she knew she had a very long and difficult night of physics homework ahead of her.

As the bell dismissed everyone from second period, she shuffled out of the classroom and into the crowded hallway. She really didn't feel like talking to anybody, so she moved along near the wall, looking down as if she found people's feet really interesting. Then she smacked into someone. "Hey!" she cried out as she jerked her head up to see who she just collided with.

"Oh, I'm sorry! Are you okay?"

Elizabeth's heart began to beat more quickly and her stomach lurched. Of all people to run into literally, she had bumped heads with Sarah Wilson. "Yeah, I'm fine," she stammered. "And all my stuff is in my backpack, so I didn't drop anything. I hope you're okay, too. Well, I'd better be off. Don't want to be late for class, you know." She turned and began to walk away, but Sarah grabbed her arm to stop her.

"Wait. Please. I've been meaning to talk to you. I just didn't plan on plowing into you to do it."

Elizabeth studied Sarah. She had a genuine smile on her freckled face, so it didn't seem like she was going to lash out at her for dating her ex-boyfriend. Her blue eyes implored her to stay. Elizabeth glanced at her arm. Sarah was still grasping it, as if she were desperate to keep her from bolting. After sizing her up, Elizabeth decided that she'd talk to her. She could always cut the conversation short and leave.

"Well, okay," she said reluctantly. "But I really don't want to be late for class. I've already been late for one today."

"No problem. We still have five minutes, and we'll walk toward your class as we talk. I don't care if I'm late for next period. This is really important; biology can wait. Which way is your class?"

Elizabeth nodded to the hallway on their left. "That way."

Sarah turned in the direction that she indicated and immediately began talking. "You're dating Brad Evans." It was a statement rather than a question.

"Yeah." Elizabeth's palms instantly became sweaty. She didn't really want to say much more. She didn't know what Sarah wanted, and she didn't want to say too much.

"You probably know that Brad and I used to go out. We went together for two years. We broke up this past July."

"Yeah, I know." She was becoming more uneasy. She just wanted to reach her classroom so she'd have an excuse to duck away, but the hallway seemed to stretch on into infinity.

Sarah seemed to sense her uneasiness. "Look, Elizabeth, you don't have to worry that I'm still after Brad and that I'm here to threaten you to stay away from my man. In fact, that's the last thing in the world I would want." Elizabeth looked at her sideways but remained silent as she continued. "We don't have much time, so I'm just going to get to the point: stay away from Brad! But not because I want him back," she added quickly when Elizabeth shot her a nasty look and began to turn around. "Stay away from him because he's a jerk. He's a control freak, he is mean, and he is rough when he doesn't get his way." She paused to let Elizabeth think about this, and then went on. "I can tell by the look on your face that you don't believe me, but please listen. I'll bet he's been pretty sweet to you, hasn't he? Saying all sorts of nice things about how he's crazy about you? You don't have to tell me, but just think about it. I'm sure he means it, but there's more to Brad than just what's on the surface. Have you noticed his temper yet? He can be pretty quick to anger. That's a warning sign, Elizabeth. Pay attention to it. Underneath his smooth-talking façade, Brad Evans is a creep. Get away from him while you still can. Brad had me trapped for a long time. I went through two years of hell with him, Elizabeth, and I lost a lot. We don't have time now for me to tell you what he did, but I will talk to you any time you'd like. Please let me talk to you. I don't want to see you become his victim. You've got too much to lose. Be careful, Elizabeth, or Brad will destroy you. Please think twice before becoming too involved with him."

Through Sarah's entire lecture, Elizabeth grew more and more angry. By the time Sarah finished, she was so livid that she could feel the tops of her ears burning and knew they were beet red. "You're way out of line, Sarah," she fumed. "Brad is a great guy and we care about each other, not that it's any of your business. Know what I think? I think you're jealous that Brad and I are together. I bet he dumped you and you can't get over it. Well, do something to get over it because Brad and I are together now." With that, she turned and marched into her classroom.

"Elizabeth, no! Please listen to me..." Sarah began but trailed off when the bell rang.

Elizabeth sat frozen in her seat, her back stiff, and refused to move a muscle, much less turn around and look at the door. After five minutes had passed, she figured that Sarah could not possibly be standing outside the classroom anymore, so she relaxed. She risked a quick peek back at the door and discovered that she was right—Sarah was gone.

I can't believe that Sarah Wilson! How gutsy! To pretend to be all sweet and sincere. Ha! And to think that I almost fell for it! How dumb does she think I am, anyway, to believe that stupid "Brad-the-creep" story? The nerve of some people! Boy, she really needs to get over Brad and get a life. Wait until I tell Meg about this!

No, I don't want to tell Meg about this. She'll probably keep going on and on about it and probably make up all sorts of dumb stuff like she always does. Brad is right—Meg is too flighty. Besides, Meg probably won't speak to me after this morning, anyway. And I hope she doesn't. It will make it easier to avoid her. I wish the world would just go away and leave Brad and me alone.

Elizabeth fumed for the entire period. The bell jolted her out of her reverie. With a sigh, she copied down the homework assignment from the board, thinking that she'd have difficult homework in yet another subject that night.

Later that evening, she found that her difficult homework was actually a relief. It gave her an excuse to stay in her room and avoid her parents. When she came home from tennis practice, her mom had been there to greet her, as usual. But this time, her cheerful chatter had annoyed her.

"Hi, Lizzie! How was your day, sweetheart?" Even her standard greeting had bothered her. *Does she have to be so darn cheerful all the time?* she had thought.

"Fine, I guess," she had replied vaguely.

"Lizzie! You don't sound fine. Let's talk. What's up?"

"Look, Mom, I'm really tired, and I have a ton of homework for tomorrow. I'd just like to go to my room and get to work if that's okay. I'm not even hungry for supper. I've got so much to do. Can I just go get started?" She had been annoyed that she, a junior in high school, had to ask her mother's permission to go to her room and do homework.

"Sure, honey. If that's what you need to do." Her mom had sounded a bit disappointed, but she had smiled at Elizabeth and touched her shoulder. "Let me know if you need anything."

At that point, Elizabeth had shrugged away and murmured, "Thanks." Then she went to her room and shut the door.

Elizabeth had a difficult time doing her homework that night. For one thing, she was concentrating more on her texts with Brad than on her assignments. For another, the material was hard because she hadn't paid much attention in her classes. Further, she kept replaying scenes from the day in her mind. As she did this, she concluded that she was really glad to have Brad in her life. Everyone else was beginning to annoy her beyond belief. Jealous Sarah Wilson had been way out of line today, and Brad was certainly right about Meg. Elizabeth hadn't noticed before, but Meg's overly bubbly behavior and inane chatter were obnoxious. She was beginning to think Brad was right about her parents, too. Thinking about how they always treated her, always asked about people and activities in her life, forcing her to stay home on school nights, and giving her a curfew—they really were treating her as if she were in grade school.

Maybe it was because her schoolwork frustrated her, or maybe she was exhausted from tennis practice. She really didn't understand why, but she went to bed irritated at everyone in the world except Brad.

CHAPTER 8

Meg watched in shocked disbelief on Tuesday morning as her best friend turned on her heel and rushed away. Little waves of hurt moved through her body. She had arrived at school early that morning to wait for Lizzie. She usually saw her before school, but today she wanted to make sure she did. She just couldn't risk missing her today. Lizzie's behavior was so strange yesterday that Meg worried all night that something was seriously wrong with her friend.

For as long as she had known her, Lizzie was always easygoing and relaxed. She was willing to bet her life savings—all $305 of it—that Lizzie had never been tense nor had she ever snapped at anyone in her life. But yesterday, Meg saw a very tense, snappy Lizzie. She had been absolutely stunned at Lizzie's reaction to her light-hearted joking before English class. All she had done was bring up a long-standing joke about herself and Coach Thompson, one that Lizzie always used to tease her about, but Lizzie was clearly annoyed. Then she had pretended that Meg wasn't even there for the entire duration of class. To top it all off, every time Meg had tried to approach her at tennis practice, Lizzie had found something extremely important to do, like picking up a tennis ball, and walked away. Then at night, either her phone was off or she was ignoring her.

Meg had rushed to school this morning, hoping for the chance to take Lizzie aside and have a long chat with her. Something had to be terribly wrong with her friend. Was something wrong at home? Was one of her parents dying? Meg figured it had to be something major to make Lizzie act so out of character.

But now she wasn't so sure. Lizzie had clearly snubbed her this morning, and it hurt. She wasn't quite sure why, but Elizabeth was definitely annoyed with her. *Well, just fine, Elizabeth. You may be dating the hottest guy in school, but that doesn't give you the right to be so snotty. Who needs you, anyway? I'm going to start hanging around more with my other friends who are more fun.*

With that thought, Meg instantly thought of Jenny. She, Elizabeth, and Jenny had known each other since grade school and had always gotten along. The three of them would hang out together sometimes. But close friendships of three were hard to pull off, and when it came right down to it, Meg and Elizabeth were the closest. They had known each other even longer than they had known Jenny, and had had a bond since toddlerhood. But things were obviously changing. Meg and Elizabeth seemed to be growing apart, and Meg had been spending more time with Jenny lately. They had two classes and lunch together, and to their teachers' annoyance, usually spent the two class periods joking and giggling over something. Lunch was no different, except for the fact that they didn't get in trouble there.

Jenny really is fun to be around, thought Meg. *Actually, I'd like to get to know her better. We haven't really done anything together, just the two of us, outside of school. I think I could have more fun with her than I do with Elizabeth. She can be so stuffy. Jenny's anything but stuffy!*

Upon realizing that she certainly wasn't friendless just because she and Elizabeth were growing apart, Meg's spirits brightened. She swung her backpack over her shoulder, adjusted her ponytail, and went to her first period class. She smiled as she walked in the door and found Jenny already there.

"Morning, Jen."

"Hey, Meg. Cute hat. I like the way it looks with your ponytail, too."

Meg grinned from ear to ear. Elizabeth hated hats, and always told Meg as much. "Thanks! I could wear a hat every day if people at school wouldn't think I was a complete dork. What are you doing this weekend?"

"I don't know. I guess I really haven't thought about it yet. My parents and sister are going out of town, but I'm not. I probably won't do much of anything. What about you?"

"Hey, I just got a great idea! You don't want to sit at home alone all weekend—how boring. Want to come stay at my house? The only thing I have going is the tennis meet on Saturday. Other than that, we could order pizzas and rent movies that are so stupid they're funny and just hang out. What do you think?"

"Are you serious?"

"Of course."

"I think it sounds fun! I'd better check it out with my parents, but I'm sure they won't mind. They know you and stuff, so they won't freak out about it being dangerous."

"Great! I can't wait!"

The bell interrupted them, but it didn't stop them. Meg and Jenny spent most of the class period making up stuff about what they would do, until Jenny said something particularly funny and Meg laughed aloud. At that point, the teacher moved Meg to a desk across the room. Meg didn't mind, though. She was too excited about her weekend to let anything get her down.

Meg and Jenny were unable to talk again until lunch. When they did, the topic of Elizabeth came up. "Look over there, Meg." Jenny took a bite of her hamburger and nodded to her left. "It's Elizabeth and Brad at their table. I thought they were going to join us."

"I guess not," Meg replied coolly as she poked at her food with her fork.

"Why not?"

"Who knows? It seems like they're too good to associate with anyone else." She had been stewing about Elizabeth's behavior despite her good mood about Jenny, and her hurt was turning into anger. "What is with her lately, anyway? Does she ever talk to you?"

"Not really, but then I guess I don't get a chance to see her very often. We don't have any classes together, and she sits with Brad during lunch."

"That's my point!" exclaimed Meg. "She's always with Brad. And you know, that's fine. I mean, if I had a really cool boyfriend I would want to spend time with him, too, but that doesn't mean that I would completely ignore the rest of the world. She acts like no one else even exists. She thinks she's so great just because she's dating Brad Evans."

"Maybe that will change. Their relationship is still pretty new," Jenny rationalized. "She's probably just caught up in it right now, but that's bound to wear off."

"Maybe, but I still think she's become stuck-up. How annoying!"

Since Meg was clearly upset about Elizabeth, Jenny switched the subject. "Speaking of annoying, what did you think of that chemistry test? That was the worst! I'll be lucky if I get a C."

"Oh, man, that was nasty! Jenny, I'm really worried about it. I don't think I passed it. My grade was already low to begin with; I'm getting a D! I could get kicked off the tennis team. When my parents find out about my grade and the team, they're going to kill me. I just have to bring my grade up."

"Why don't we work on chemistry after school a few times a week?" suggested Jenny. "Maybe by putting our heads together we can figure the stuff out and raise our grades. What do you think?"

At the sound of the bell, Meg stood up and picked up her tray. Everyone was starting to file out of the lunchroom and back to their classes. "That's a great idea. I'll try anything to get my grade up."

As Meg walked through the crowded lunchroom with Jenny, her elbow bumped someone else's tray. "Whoops. Sorry," she mumbled over her shoulder without really looking back. She was too engrossed in her conversation with Jenny to notice that the person whose tray she bumped was Elizabeth.

CHAPTER 9

On Thursday evening, Elizabeth threw open the front door and ran into the house. She dumped her tennis racket and book bag on the hall table as she ran straight for the kitchen. "Mom! Mom! Oh, my gosh! Brad's going to be here any minute and I don't have time to get ready. Coach Thompson kept us late to prepare for Saturday's meet. I ran all the way home. What are you making for supper?" She was still out of breath from her sprint home, so she only managed to get a few words out at a time. After inquiring about dinner, she bent over to catch her breath.

"For goodness' sakes, Elizabeth, slow down! Why on earth didn't you get a ride from Meg?"

At that, Elizabeth stood up. To avoid looking her mom in the eye, she walked to the fridge to get a glass of water. "I think Meg had somewhere she had to be right away. You know how that goes. Anyway, the food smells great. What is it?"

"Roast chicken with vegetables, and I even baked! I made homemade bread and angel food cake for strawberry shortcake. I thought it would be a nice, safe meal—one that anyone would like. What do you think?"

"Sounds good to me. I hope Brad likes it." When she saw that her mom was beginning to look worried, she added, "How could he not like it? You're a great cook!"

Just then the doorbell rang, sending Elizabeth into a panic. "Oh, no! Brad is here!" She grabbed one of her mom's silver pots and used it as a mirror. With great dismay she groaned. "I've never looked worse in my life! Just look at my hair, plastered all over my forehead. My face is red, and I feel sweaty and stinky. Oh, I'm so mad at Coach Thompson! Why did he have to keep us late tonight of all nights?"

"Elizabeth," her mother responded, "you look fine. So what if you're just getting home from tennis practice? Do you think Brad will really care? You should see how guys look after football practice. Now calm down and answer the door. I've got to check supper."

Elizabeth left the kitchen and headed back down the hallway. Her tennis shoes were loud on the hardwood floor, and she just knew that Brad could hear her. *Great. Not only do I look and smell like a sweaty horse, but I sound like one, too.* She forced herself to smile and look relaxed as she opened the door. "Hi, Brad!"

Brad just stared at her for a few moments. Finally, he spoke. "Hi. Jeez, don't you shower and change after practice?"

"Usually, but I just got home. Thompson let us out late."

"Now I understand why girls never like anyone to see them after they work out."

"Yeah," she murmured, embarrassed. "I'll take you to the kitchen so you can visit with my mom, and I'll run up and change. It won't take long."

"No way. I don't know your mom well enough to sit there alone with her. You'll just have to stay like that, I guess." His tone was harsh, and he stared at her with disapproval.

Elizabeth knew that her cheeks were bright red; she could feel them burning. Before, though, they had been flushed from her difficult practice and her run home. Now, they were hot with embarrassment. *I must look even worse than I thought. First, I act as though we're in grade school, making Brad come to my house for a date. Then I greet him for our "date" looking like yesterday's garbage. I'm surprised he's even sticking around.*

"Brad, I'm—" She stopped short when she saw her father walking up the sidewalk. *Oh, please let this night go well,* she thought as he introduced himself to her boyfriend.

She needn't have worried, for the dinner went very well. Brad was as charming to Elizabeth's parents as he usually was to her, complimenting her mother on the meal and showing interest in her father's line of work. Brad politely answered her parents' questions about school, the football team, and his plans for the future. By the end of the dinner, Elizabeth was completely relaxed. Studying her parents' expressions and listening to their comments, she guessed that they approved wholeheartedly of Brad. When her father dismissed them to the family room and informed them that he and her mother would stay out of their way for the rest of the evening, Elizabeth knew that Brad had won them over.

When she and Brad entered the family room, Elizabeth plopped down cross-legged on the couch, heaved a sigh of relief, and exclaimed, "Free at last!" After a pause, she added, "That went great, don't you think?"

Brad remained standing. "Great?" he asked sarcastically.

"Don't you think so?"

"If you consider getting grilled about everything under the sun great, then I guess it did. But frankly, I was getting sick of the third degree."

"What do you mean?"

"Come on, Elizabeth! Don't tell me you didn't notice. All they did during the entire meal was question me. I'm surprised they didn't fingerprint me for a background check with the FBI."

Elizabeth didn't want him to think her parents didn't approve of him. She was afraid that he might decide that she just wasn't worth the hassle and find a girlfriend with less interfering parents. "Oh, no, Brad. They weren't trying to give you the third degree. They were just trying to make conversation. Honest."

"Elizabeth, it was like the Spanish Inquisition."

She didn't know how to respond. She tucked her knees up under her chest and self-consciously ran her fingers through her hair. Doing so reminded her that she looked terrible. *What am I going to do now?* she thought. *I've really screwed up tonight. I don't want him to break up with me, but I don't know what to do to fix things.* She bit her lip and looked down at her socks.

At that, Brad walked over and sat beside her on the couch. He reached over, put his hand under her chin, and gently turned her head until she was looking at him. "Hey, don't feel bad. It's not your fault your parents are so controlling. Look, I can handle them. Wasn't I great at dinner tonight?" She couldn't argue with that. She nodded, and Brad continued. "I'm just afraid that I won't measure up to their expectations. I hate it when people question me like that because I always seem to fall short of what they want. I guess I'm worried, too, because I figure if my own father doesn't want me, why should yours? I'd die if your parents decided that you couldn't see me anymore."

As always, he completely overwhelmed her with his sweetness. She moved closer to him and leaned against him. "Brad, that won't happen; I wouldn't let it anyway. I care about you and I am going to continue to see you no matter what anyone says—including my parents."

"Liz, that means so much to hear you say that." They sat silently for a few minutes, and then he spoke again. "But Elizabeth, next time we get together, make sure you look presentable, okay?"

She pulled back from him to see that he was looking at her, straight-faced. She couldn't tell if he was joking or serious, but she didn't want to ruin the moment by asking, so she just grinned and hit him with one of the sofa pillows. She jumped out of the way before he could retaliate and spied her *Great Expectations* script sitting on an end table. "Hey, Brad, will you help me rehearse lines for tomorrow's audition? I've been practicing every night this week, but I still feel like I need work."

"Are you really going through with that, Elizabeth? You know I don't want you to do this. It'll just take time away from us."

"That's so sweet, but we've already been through this. In a few weeks tennis will be over, and then I'll only have the play to concentrate on. Then it won't be any different for us than it is now. That is, of course, if I even make the play. Now here." She tossed him the script. "Look at pages fourteen and fifteen. I've highlighted all of the lines for Mrs. Joe; that's the part I'm auditioning for. I've pretty much got the lines on those two pages memorized, but I need to practice my delivery. Just read the lines around mine, and I'll fill in."

Brad sighed and glared at her, but he picked up the script and began to read. Elizabeth didn't care that he mumbled them in a monotone voice; she just needed someone to speak the lines so she could respond. After they went through the two pages, she turned hopeful eyes to him. "Well? What did you think? I think it still needs some work, but I'm feeling more comfortable with the lines now."

"I don't think you should get yourself too pumped up about being in the play."

Elizabeth was confused. "Why not?"

"Well, I'm not an expert in theatre, but you really didn't sound that great."

Her heart sank, and she felt foolish for practicing her lines in front of him. "I know I'm not going to win any awards. I thought I could make the school play, though. I'll just have to practice a lot more before tomorrow after school, I guess. Thanks for helping me." Brad had placed the script on the couch between them. She snatched it and put it back on the end table, and then quickly changed the subject. "Now that we're several weeks into the school year, I hear that some of the clubs are getting started. Are you still planning to join any?"

Brad perked up. "Yeah, I have to. I need to be active in school in order to be considered for big scholarships from most colleges. There's a weightlifting club that I want to join, and I'm considering the German club. I've only taken two years of German, and some schools like to see athletes have more foreign language than that. I figure it'll look good if I belong to the German club, then they'll see I've had more opportunities to use the language. That's what I'm hoping, anyway."

They chatted about school and their classes, and Brad's upcoming basketball season for a while. When the subject of math and science came up, Elizabeth mentioned that she planned to join the computer and environmental clubs. She was shocked when Brad flew off the handle at this announcement.

"Absolutely not, Elizabeth!" He raised his voice, but quickly lowered it when Elizabeth put her finger to her lips and gestured toward the door, indicating that her parents would easily hear him yelling. He spoke quietly, but his face remained red. "You are really something else, you know that? I thought you cared about me and wanted this relationship to succeed." He folded his arms across his chest and turned away.

She was quick to reassure him. "Of course I do, Brad! You are the best thing in my life."

"Well, it sure doesn't seem that way. You waste so much time playing tennis, trying to be good for the varsity team." He sneered the word "varsity" so it sounded like something bad. "You want to be in the play, although I don't know why. You really can't act. Now you want to join two clubs at school. Are you even interested in spending any time with me at all?"

Elizabeth quickly decided that the computer club and the environmental club were not worth losing her boyfriend over. She put her hand on his shoulder and apologized. "You're right, Brad. I'm really sorry. I didn't even think about it that way. Since I want to be an engineer, I had always planned to be really involved in math, science, and computers in high school. I really didn't think about how it would affect us; I'd much rather spend time with you. I won't join either club, I promise."

Brad turned back toward her, smiled, and took her in his arms. "I'm glad to hear that, Liz. I guess sometimes you really don't think, do you? At least you came to your senses about this. I forgive you."

Her shoulders relaxed. She was so relieved that Brad wasn't upset with her that she didn't even realize he had not said he would give up his clubs, too.

——•——

Late Saturday afternoon, Elizabeth was ecstatic. Her heart raced, and she was so pumped up that she felt as if she could run a marathon in about ten minutes. She bounced on her toes and grinned through Coach Thompson's entire post-meet talk.

"Excellent, excellent job today, girls! The Chesterville Bears are ranked number one in the state, and we are most definitely advancing to the state competition. Girls, what you did today is almost unheard of. Every single one of you—varsity and JV—defeated your opponent. We didn't lose a single match today, and Elizabeth here didn't lose a single game! Way to go, Liz!" The coach gave her a high five and continued. "That doesn't mean that we can slack off now until state, though. We have several tough meets ahead of us, and if we let up now, we jeopardize our chances of taking state."

He went on to lay out exactly what was in store for the team in the upcoming weeks, and Elizabeth got goose bumps. *Wow! Winning the state championship is now a strong possibility! We're really pulling together as a team, and I think we can do it. I can see all of us working hard to win! Go Bears!*

When Coach Thompson dismissed the team for the remainder of the weekend, Elizabeth turned to leave and found Brad waiting for her by the fence. Since she wasn't leaving with Meg, she ran right over to him. In fact, she and Meg hadn't spoken to each other lately.

"Brad!" she shouted as she dashed toward him. "We swept the meet, and I didn't lose a single game today!"

"That's great, Liz," he said flatly. "Jeez, your coach is long-winded. I've been waiting forever."

"Oh, I know! I was dying to get out of there, but it was okay listening to him, too. We're making plans for the state tournament!"

"Yeah, but doesn't it drive you crazy that he drones on so long? I think he just likes to hear his own voice. You and I have better things to do than wait around for Thompson to finish babbling. Speaking of which, let's go get ready for tonight."

"All right! What should we do? How about Grizzly's?"

"No. Too crowded."

They discussed their plans as he drove her home. It was clear that they definitely weren't going to Grizzly's. They decided to go to Putter Around, a miniature golf course and go-cart track, and then out for pizza. By the time they reached Elizabeth's house, they were both excited about the evening.

"I'll pick you up in an hour," he informed her. "Hey, why don't you wear that tan miniskirt with the little white tank top—the one with the spaghetti straps? You look sexy in that." He winked at her.

Elizabeth's cheeks flushed with pleasure. "Thanks. But that's not a very good outfit for miniature golf. I think I'll save that for next time and find something else you'll like this time."

"Out of the question. I said I like the miniskirt and tank top. I'm taking you out for a fun evening, and you don't want to make me happy?"

"That's not it at all. I didn't think about it that way. Of course I'll wear the outfit you like. I want to make you as happy as you make me."

"That's my girl! Go make yourself gorgeous. See you in an hour."

Brad returned an hour later and waited in her driveway. After about ten minutes, the front door opened and Elizabeth trotted down the sidewalk. She opened the car door and hopped in, fastened her seat belt, tucked her hair behind her ears, and then turned to Brad with a smile. "Sorry it took me so long."

"What happened to the outfit I asked you to wear?" His voice was low, and it was clear that he was not happy.

"Oh, that." She chuckled. "Actually, that's why I'm late. You see, after I showered and changed, I realized I was incredibly thirsty from tennis today, so I decided to have some orange juice. I filled a huge glass then dropped it on myself! My white tank top is now orange. The skirt didn't fare any better, so I had to find a different miniskirt. Can you believe it?"

"Not really. You did it on purpose, didn't you? So you didn't have to wear it?"

"Of course not! Like I said, it was an accident. It that so hard to believe?"

"I guess with you anything's possible, isn't it? I thought that only little kids spilled on themselves. How did you make the varsity tennis team if you're that clumsy?"

"Gosh, Brad, it was just an accident. What's the big deal?"

"Nothing, I guess. I'm just disappointed. I was looking forward to that outfit. You know, you're lucky to have me. Most people wouldn't put up with someone who spills all over themselves before a date."

They drove to Putter Around in silence, and Elizabeth glanced nervously at Brad from time to time. He sat with both hands gripping the steering wheel, staring straight ahead, his face frozen in a scowl. Elizabeth grew nervous. *I've really done it this time. Brad is probably sorry that he even asked me out in the first place. Senior guys want girls who are mature. I bet he's irritated because sometimes I seem so immature. I used to hang around flighty Meg. My stupid parents don't allow me the freedom I deserve, which ends up restricting not just me but Brad, too. Then I go and do dumb stuff like spilling juice on myself. Not only that, but I made Brad sit in the driveway waiting for me for ten minutes. I also kept him waiting for me after my meet today. No wonder he's annoyed. I'm lucky he hasn't broken up with me already.*

After what seemed like hours, they reached Putter Around. Brad jerked the car into the parking lot and screeched to a halt. Before Elizabeth could even unfasten her seat belt, he jumped out of the car, slammed the door, and headed up the sidewalk toward the mini golf course. Not wanting to anger him further, Elizabeth hurried out of the car and ran to catch up with him. She reached him just as he was getting their clubs and balls. She hid her discomfort behind a smile and a cheerful voice. "Hey, thanks, Brad! Let's go play some golf. You're so incredible; I'll bet you're even great at this!"

Much to her dismay, he only shrugged. He shoved one of the clubs and a ball at her and marched off toward the first hole.

Brad sulked through the entire course. Occasionally Elizabeth would compliment him on a shot or try to make a joke out of one of the course props, but eventually she gave up. They played the whole game in silence—not once did he look directly at her.

Elizabeth watched him play. He would hit the ball—sometimes too hard—walk up, and hit it again. Every once in a while he would curse at a bad shot. After he putted the ball into a hole, he would reach down, snatch it up, and stomp off to the next hole without waiting to see what Elizabeth was doing. When he finished the last hole, he brushed past her and muttered, "Come on. Let's go. I'm hungry." Even though she hadn't yet finished, she picked up her ball, turned in her equipment, and followed him to the car.

By the time they reached the restaurant and sat down at a booth, Elizabeth felt sick and dizzy. Her hands were clammy, and her mouth was so dry she had difficulty swallowing. She had really done it this time, and now she was afraid that Brad was going to break up with her. As she waited for him to decide what kind of pizza they were going to have, her eyes welled up with tears. She tried unsuccessfully to keep her voice even when she spoke.

"Brad, I'm sorry. Please, please don't be mad at me. I don't want you to break up with me. I'll be better, I promise."

He put the menu down and looked at her. "Oh, Liz, sometimes you frustrate me so much, but you are so gorgeous. I love the way you tuck your beautiful hair behind your ears. Your big brown eyes drive me wild. You are so sexy, and usually you're great to be around." He paused, and when she still looked forlorn, he came around to her side of the booth. He slid in beside her and put his arm around her. "Even though you do stupid stuff sometimes, I really am crazy about you, Liz. I don't want to lose you, either." Ignoring the fact that they were in a restaurant, he leaned down and kissed her.

She wrapped her arms around his neck and kissed him back. She was so lost in the moment that she thought of nothing but Brad's kiss until she heard someone clear his throat. She opened her eyes and stared right at their waiter.

Feeling Elizabeth tense, Brad pulled away. Laughing, he said to the waiter, "I guess we kinda forgot why we're here. Pizza was the furthest thing from my mind."

Brad ordered a large pizza. "I got us a large, but don't eat too much," he told Elizabeth after the waiter had gone. "You're sexy now, but I want you to stay that way." Then he bent down and kissed her again.

They had a much nicer time at the restaurant than they had at the miniature golf course. They were both relaxed and happy. After the meal, Brad excused himself to use the restroom. While he was gone, two guys from Elizabeth's physics class arrived at the restaurant. Elizabeth waved to them, and they came over to chat.

"Hi, Elizabeth. What are you doing here?"

"Hey, Jake. Hi, Matt. Brad and I are on a date. I'm just waiting for him; he's in the bathroom. What are you doing here?"

"Just hanging out. We were at Grizzly's, but we wanted some real food, so we left," replied Jake. "Boy, you are the envy of lots of girls to be dating Brad Evans. What's he got that the rest of us don't, anyway?" Before she could reply, Jake continued. "How are you doing in physics, Elizabeth? Man, that class is a killer!"

"I'm getting a B, but I would like it to be an A. I need to spend more time studying. Oh, here comes Brad! Why don't you guys sit down? We're done eating, but we'll hang around for awhile." Elizabeth turned to address Brad as he approached. "Brad, do you know Matt and Jake?"

He smiled and greeted them, but then quickly said, "Come on, Elizabeth. We've got to go."

"Brad—" She started to protest, but Brad stopped her.

"I said let's go, Liz." Much to her surprise, he reached down, grabbed her arm, and yanked her out of the booth.

"Well, I guess we're off to other things," she managed to say to Jake and Matt.

"Right. See you in physics," Matt replied.

Once in the parking lot, Brad gripped Elizabeth's arm forcefully and pulled her toward his car. He was moving so quickly and tugging her so hard that she had to scramble on her tiptoes to keep up. When she tried to jerk free, he tightened his grip and glared at her.

"Ouch! Brad, that hurts! Let go!"

Brad ignored her.

"Brad! I said let go of me!"

He stomped until they reached his car, then he flung her against the side and stared at her. He did not let go of her arm. "What were you doing in there?" he yelled.

Elizabeth's heart was racing. Brad was really frightening her. Her arm throbbed, her back hurt from hitting the car, and now he was shouting at her. What really confused her was that she had absolutely no idea what had set him off like this. "What in the world are you talking about?"

"Don't play dumb with me, Elizabeth. I know that you're not the brightest person in the world, but you can't be totally stupid. You know exactly what I'm talking about!"

She looked around nervously. Was anyone watching this? Thankfully, the parking lot was relatively dark—there were only a few lights placed far apart—and it seemed devoid of people. "No, Brad, I don't. Why don't you fill me in?"

"Why were you sitting with those guys when you're supposed to be out on a date with me?"

She looked at her boyfriend in disbelief. Was he serious? A shooting pain in her arm reminded her that he was still holding onto her. She tried to wrench herself free, but he wouldn't let go. She glanced down at her arm, and when she looked back up at Brad, her eyes were filled with fury. "Let go of me right now, Brad." Her voice was low and she spoke very slowly. It must have intimidated him, because he let go. "You are crazy. Those are friends of mine from physics class. I do not see how in the world they are threatening to you or our date. This date is over, Brad. Take me home right now. And frankly, I don't think I want to go out with you at all anymore." Elizabeth said nothing more. She quietly slid past Brad, walked around his car, and got in.

She stared straight ahead, heart racing, waiting for him to drive her home. She sat immobile for what seemed like an eternity. She shifted uncomfortably, sorry she had worn a miniskirt; her legs were sticking to the vinyl car seat. Her shoulders were beginning to feel stiff.

After a few more minutes, Elizabeth got back out of the car. Brad was still standing exactly where he had been. She could see only the back of his head because it was bowed, and he was staring at the ground. She was afraid to remind him that she had a curfew, but she had to if she didn't want to be late.

"Brad?" she began. "I really need to get home; it's close to my curfew." She figured that he would say something sarcastic, but he didn't. In fact, he didn't say anything at all. He didn't even move. She walked back around the car and approached him. "Brad?" she repeated.

He looked up at her, and her eyes widened in surprise. He was crying! He gently took her hands in his. "Liz, oh, Liz, I'm so sorry. Please forgive me." His voice cracked, and Elizabeth's heart melted. "I guess I went nuts in there because I don't want to lose you to another guy. You mean so much to me. All I want is to be with you. I just want everyone else to go away sometimes. Please, please, don't leave me.

"Elizabeth, you are the only person I really have in my life. My mom has to work all the time just so she can support me, and I know she resents that. She acts like she'll be glad when I'm off to college and out of her hair. My dad and my little brother want nothing to do with me. After they left, I figured that I'd still see them a lot, you know; but they never call, never ask me to come see them. I called a couple of times, but they always had some excuse not to see me. Now I don't even bother to call. It hurts too much to have them say no.

"Now you want to leave me, too, because I'm such a jerk. I know that you have every right to leave, but I don't want you to. I'd die if I lost you, too. Liz, please stay in my life." Brad had been looking down at the ground, but now he looked straight into her eyes. Her heart went out to him as his green eyes bore imploringly into hers. They stood like that for a few minutes, each staring into the other's eyes. At last Elizabeth spoke.

"Oh, Brad, I'm sorry, too. I was wrong to invite Jake and Matt to sit with us. I should have remembered that I was on a date with you, not them. You mean so much to me, and I feel like the luckiest girl in school to be dating you. I really don't want to break up with you. I'm so sorry I said that."

At that, Brad pulled her close and kissed her. His kiss wasn't gentle like it had been in the restaurant. It was filled with relief and passion, and it made Elizabeth feel tingly all over. With what seemed like great effort, he pulled away and just held her. "Thank you, Elizabeth. Thank you for staying with me. I love you."

Her stomach jumped into her throat. *Brad loves me!* "I love you, too, Brad."

"I hate to break the moment, Liz, but I'm afraid it's past your curfew."

Elizabeth turned on her watch's light so she could accurately see the time. Brad was right; at this moment, she was exactly twenty minutes late, and it would take at least fifteen minutes to drive home. "Shoot. I guess you'd better take me home. I'm sure my parents will be furious, but you know what? I don't care! They're just going to have to deal with it. I'm tired of their controlling me all the time. Now come on, Brad Evans, take me home, but don't drive too fast!"

CHAPTER 10

On Monday morning, Meg slinked into her third period class and slumped down in her desk with a small sigh. She took out her notebook and then just sat, waiting for her class to begin. She knew that she still had several minutes before the bell would ring. Normally, she would be out in the hallway chatting and laughing with somebody—probably Jenny—but today she really didn't feel like it. *It's not that I don't like Jenny,* she told herself. *In fact, I've found that I like her a lot. We have tons of fun together. But sometimes...I don't know. Sometimes I guess I just miss Elizabeth. How could she just completely dump me like she did, after we've been so close for so long? I wish that things were still the same between us, especially today. As much as I like Jenny, talking to her just isn't the same as talking to Lizzie."*

I wish I could confide in someone about my problem. I hate science. I really can't stand biology especially, and the thought of being a doctor makes me sick. Mom and Dad won't let it drop, though. They really freaked out when they got a note from Mr. Jenkins telling them that I'm getting a D in bio. I don't know what's worse—the other night when they yelled at me about my grade or this morning when they gave me a "pep" talk about being a doctor. Sure, I could mention it to Jenny, but she really wouldn't understand quite like Lizzie.

Meg sat with her elbow on her desk, hunched over with her head resting on her hand, and stared down at her open notebook. She wasn't in a position to notice if someone had approached her, so she was startled when she heard a voice ask, "Meg?"

She looked up in surprise and was further shocked to see Sarah Wilson. Although they saw each other every day in biology, they never spoke to each other. Part of the reason was because Meg was slightly uncomfortable around Sarah. After all, Sarah was Brad's old girlfriend, and Meg's former best friend was now dating Brad. But another part was because Meg just didn't know Sarah that well; she was pretty quiet and usually kept to herself. She wasn't involved in anything and didn't seem to have a lot of friends. What in the world did Sarah want to talk to her about? Her curiosity kicked in, and she instantly perked up.

"Hey, Sarah. What's up?"

"Meg, I really need to talk to you. It's very important, and I'd like to talk to you soon. Not now, though. Class is going to start in a couple of minutes, and I need more time than that. I was wondering if we could talk during lunch today."

"Sure. What's it about?" Meg was dying to know. It seemed so out of character for Sarah to do this, but she didn't know much about her, so maybe it was in keeping with her character after all.

Suddenly, the bell rang. "I'll tell you at lunch. Meet me by the cafeteria doors right after fifth period. See you then!" With a little wave at Meg, Sarah hurried off to her seat.

Mr. Jenkins had started class, but Meg wasn't paying attention. She was too lost in thought about Sarah. *She seems okay. She's nice, cute, and stylish, and for a long time she was dating the most popular guy in school. I wonder why she keeps to herself so much?* Unable to come up with an answer to her own question, Meg dismissed that thought and spent the rest of the class period ignoring Mr. Jenkins. She just couldn't stand biology. She amused herself by making up stories about what Sarah might talk about during lunch.

Third period went by quickly, but fourth and fifth periods seemed to drag on forever. Finally, the bell rang to dismiss fifth period, and Meg charged out of the classroom and flew down the hallway to the cafeteria. She didn't even bother to drop off her morning books and pick up her afternoon ones at her locker; she didn't want to risk missing Sarah.

She stood in front of the cafeteria and watched the crowd of students pass through the doors. At last she spotted Sarah, who had stepped away from the crowd and seemed to be looking for her. "Sarah! Sarah! Over here!" She had to shout over the noise of the crowd filing into the lunchroom. She stood on her toes and waved her arms above her head. Sarah looked in her direction, waved back, and began working her way over toward Meg.

"Hi, Sarah. I didn't know if you'd see me, even when I stood on my toes. Sometimes I hate being so short."

Sarah laughed. "Yeah, well, at least you don't have to worry about hitting your head as you go through doorways."

Meg laughed, too. *She seems to be easy to talk to and has a good sense of humor. I really wonder why she doesn't have lots of friends.*

She didn't realize it, but her question about Sarah was soon to be answered. They talked about school as they moved through the lunch line. When they had their trays of food, Sarah led them to a table. As soon as they sat down, Sarah looked Meg in the eyes. She held her gaze for several seconds, and then she spoke solemnly. "I need to talk to you about Elizabeth and Brad."

Meg could sense that Sarah had something very important to say. "Okay."

Sarah picked up her fork to take a bite food, but immediately put it down. Pushing her tray aside, she folded her hands on the table, looked back and Meg, and began. "Meg, I am very concerned about Elizabeth. I obviously don't know her as well as you do, but I know her enough to care about what's going to happen to her if she stays with Brad. I've had some classes with Elizabeth, and I know her from the tennis team."

Meg was puzzled; Sarah wasn't on the tennis team. She didn't say anything, but she must have looked confused because Sarah explained. "You must not remember me from tennis; I didn't know if you would. I joined the team when I was in ninth grade. I played all of my freshman year and part of my sophomore year—I quit a few weeks into the season. You were a freshman, so you probably didn't really know me and didn't even realize it when I quit. I quit the team shortly after I met Brad."

"Oh." Meg didn't want to say too much because she wasn't quite sure where Sarah was taking the conversation.

"I regret that I quit the team. I regret a lot of things about the last two years. My main regret, though, is that I ever got involved with Brad."

Now Meg did speak up. "But you guys went out for two years. You always seemed so happy, and you were the hottest couple in school. If you didn't like going out with Brad, why did you stay with him for two years?"

She smiled. "I can see why so many people like you, Meg. You're not afraid to talk about anything. You get right to the point, but you do it in a nice way that doesn't hurt people's feelings. You're right. I shouldn't have stayed with him for two years, but it's not that simple." She paused and looked down at her hands. When she looked back up, her eyes were sad and she spoke very quietly. "Brad abused me, Meg."

Meg stopped chewing. She swallowed her bite of sandwich hard. "What?"

"Brad is abusive. I didn't realize it at first; I thought he just cared about me so much that he wanted to make sure he could spend time with me. But as time went on, things got worse and worse. He controlled everything I did—and I mean everything. He said very mean things, and even got physically rough at times. But he's clever; he hid his abusiveness behind lots of sweet talk and affection. That's why I didn't realized what was happening for a while. As time went on, though, I saw his abusive side more than his sweet side. It got pretty awful.

"I was trapped in that relationship for two years; I wasn't able to get out until last summer. Things got so bad that I finally told my parents what was happening. They helped me get away from Brad. I had wanted to break up with him but was always afraid to because I knew he'd always be right there. So this past July I broke up with him, and then right away my parents took me to visit family in Washington. We figured that Brad wouldn't harass me there. After two weeks, my dad had to come back home, but my mom and I stayed there until late August. That's the only way I could get away from Brad.

"But then I started school, and I discovered that Brad was dating Elizabeth. Meg, I've been so worried about

Elizabeth. She's such a nice girl and has so much going for her. I don't want Brad to destroy her like he destroyed me—and he did destroy me. I loved playing tennis, but he convinced me to quit so I could spend more time with him. This is my senior year, and I should be on the varsity team, but it's too late. I couldn't just jump back on the team after quitting during the season two years ago.

"I really don't want to see Elizabeth go through what I did or what I'm going through now. All my activities, all my friends, went on without me. Now I'm on the outside looking in. I tried to warn Elizabeth awhile back, but she just thought I was jealous that she's dating my old boyfriend. That couldn't be further from the truth. I can't approach her again because she'll just shut me out, but I thought that maybe you could talk to her, Meg. Please, please, try to get through to her before it's too late."

Sarah stared at Meg intensely, and Meg was too stunned by what she had heard to look away. "I'll try," she whispered.

"You have to do more than that, for Elizabeth's sake," implored Sarah.

"I'll do my best," she promised, "but I don't know if she'll listen. She and I haven't exactly been speaking to each other lately."

"Oh, no. It's starting already, then. Don't you see, Meg? This is one of the ways Brad controls people. He probably made something up about you to keep you and Elizabeth apart. You can't let this stop you, Meg. You've got to warn Elizabeth. I think you should try to do it alone first, but if you don't get anywhere then we'll gang up together. Think about the way Elizabeth has always been. She's intelligent, she's athletic, she's involved in school, and she must be fun to be with or you wouldn't have been friends with her for so long. Do you want to see her destroyed by Brad Evans?"

Meg thought about many of the good times she and Elizabeth had together since they were little. She thought about all of the hopes and dreams for the future that Lizzie had confided in her through the years. Worry lines creased her forehead as she looked into Sarah's eyes. "No, I do not."

Chapter 11

Elizabeth stood in line for her lunch tray. She could barely stand still as she waited. At the end of last period, the school secretary's voice had come over the intercom and announced the cast for *Great Expectations*. Elizabeth had jumped out of her seat with joy when she heard her name called for the role of Mrs. Joe. Thankfully, Mrs. Lipkins had already finished class, or Elizabeth might have gotten into trouble.

Now she was filled with tense energy, and standing in line was practically killing her. She bounced on the balls of her feet and tapped her pen against the side of her leg. She didn't know why she was carrying a pen through the lunch line, but she was glad to have it. It gave her something to do while the line moved slowly forward.

She was excited to find Brad and share the good news, but at the same time she dreaded it. She had no idea how he would react. He was usually very supportive of her, telling her things that made her feel good. If something was bothering him, however, she knew he wouldn't be quite so supportive. Adding to her concern was the fact that he had made it perfectly clear that he did not want her in the play.

The longer she stood in line, the more nervous she became. She was very happy that she got the part, and she was looking forward to getting started, but she was not looking forward to Brad's reaction. *Oh well, I guess I'd better just get this over with.*

Oh, there he is at our table. She had finally received her tray, and she studied him carefully as she moved through the crowded cafeteria. *He's just sitting there, frowning. He hasn't even opened his lunch sack. Oh, oh. I think I'm in for it. No matter what, though, I'm not going to let him ruin my excitement about the play.*

"Brad, did you hear the announcement? I got the part of Mrs. Joe in the play!" She pretended not to notice his scowl.

"Yeah, I heard it. Big whoop. My girlfriend is in the play. Boy am I thrilled."

"You don't sound thrilled."

"Wow, you're quick. I was being sarcastic. I forgot how dumb you are. You can't even recognize sarcasm."

Elizabeth sighed. "Brad, you can't be that upset about the play."

"Yes, Elizabeth, I am. To me, it just means less time that we'll spend together."

"Brad, we've been over this before. I'll only be really swamped for a few weeks. Once tennis is over, I'll only have the play. Remember, I'm not joining any clubs or anything, so there won't be anything else to get in our way."

"I guess." He fell silent for a while. "I'm really surprised you made it," he said at last. "When you read the script for me, you were terrible. They probably didn't have enough people try out and they were really desperate. Lucky for you, huh?" He opened his lunch sack and began to eat.

Elizabeth had lost her appetite. She absentmindedly forked the food around on her plate. *Is that the only reason I made the play?* she wondered. *If I remember right, there really weren't a lot of people at the audition. What if I really am terrible and they don't actually want me but they had to pick me because there wasn't anyone else? Oh, I'll be so embarrassed at rehearsals! I'll need to work extra hard to make sure I don't totally mess things up, but I can't spend too much time on it because I don't want to make Brad mad. I truly don't want to spend a lot of time away from him. I'm glad he still wants to spend time with me. I would hate it if he were too embarrassed to see me.*

Brad finished his lunch and stood up to leave. He paused, stared at something across the lunchroom, then quickly sat back down. "Liz!"

She looked up from her tray and saw a strange, almost panic-stricken look on his face. "Brad, what is it?"

"Have you been talking to Meg lately?"

"No. You were right about her being so immature; I find her annoying. Why?"

"No reason." His expression told Elizabeth that he had a very good reason for asking such an odd question.

"Come on, Brad. You can't lie to me; I know you too well." She smiled at him and placed her hand on his. "Now tell me, why did you ask me about Meg, and why do you look so worried?"

He hesitated but then looked at Elizabeth and answered. "I just saw Meg sitting with my old girlfriend Sarah. They're not friends—they never sit together—so this makes me nervous. They must be up to something, and it can't be good. I'm afraid they might be scheming to break us up."

He seemed sad, and though she didn't want to see her boyfriend upset, she was glad he seemed worried about their relationship. "Why would they be doing that? I'm sure it's nothing, Brad. They're probably just talking about biology or something. After all, they've got that class together."

She thought that would reassure him, but instead his frown only deepened. His eyebrows knotted together, and he asked, "How do you know that?"

"I don't know. I just do."

"You have been talking to Meg, haven't you?" He glared at her, his eyes full of suspicion.

"Don't be ridiculous, Brad! Of course I haven't. I think I remember Meg saying earlier in the school year that she had biology with Sarah, that's all."

This, too, failed to comfort him. "Why were you guys talking about Sarah?"

"Gosh, Brad, I don't know. It was early in the school year; we were probably just discussing dumb stuff about our schedules. You said yourself that Meg was shallow and incapable of having an intelligent conversation. She probably just thought I'd find that to be juicy information, but I really couldn't care less. So what's the big deal if they're having lunch together today, anyway? Neither one of us has anything to do with either one of them anymore, so I don't see why it matters."

"Think about it, Elizabeth. Sarah and I went out for two years; she probably can't get over the fact that I broke up with her, and she's upset that I have a new girlfriend. And you and Meg were best friends for a long time, but now that you have me, you don't need her anymore. I'm sure they're both really jealous. I'll bet they figure that if they work together, they can break us up and solve both their problems."

Elizabeth pondered what Brad had said. "You might be right, but who cares? Let them try anything they want.

Nothing will work. I would like to think that we're too close to let them come between us."

Brad grabbed both of her hands and held them tightly in his. "I hope you mean that, Liz. I don't want to lose you. I'm already afraid that once you start the play you won't have time for me or just won't want to be with me anymore, and now I see Sarah talking to Meg. Who knows what they'll try. I can't stand the thought of losing you." He paused. "Elizabeth, please promise me that you'll stay far away from Meg. Don't give her a chance to get to you," he begged.

"I love you, Brad. I don't even like Meg anymore. I will never, ever allow her or anyone else to come between us."

Brad looked her in the eye. "Thank you, Elizabeth," he said solemnly, and then he gave her hands a final squeeze before going off to class.

———

Elizabeth had a lot on her mind as she walked to English class. She thought that she understood why Brad was always so negative when it came to the play, and it didn't bother her so much anymore. In fact, she thought it was pretty sweet that he was so concerned that the play might come between them. It felt good to have someone care that much about her. She was also quite annoyed about Meg and Sarah. How dare they try to ruin what she and Brad had! They obviously didn't realize what they were up against. The love she and Brad had for each other was too strong to let those two come between them.

When Elizabeth entered English class, she was so lost in thought that she didn't realize someone was talking to her. It took a tug at her elbow to pull her out of her reverie.

"Hey, Elizabeth. Jeez, did you even hear me?"

She turned to see who had grabbed her elbow and was surprised to find Meg standing beside her, smiling awkwardly. "Oh, hi Meg," she said coolly. "I'm sorry. Were you talking to me?"

"Yes...yeah...I, um, I was," she stammered.

Elizabeth shifted uncomfortably from one foot to the next. It was weird to feel so uneasy around Meg. They never used to have any problems with each other, but things were definitely different now. She remembered her promise to Brad and wanted to get away from Meg as soon as possible. "I guess I didn't hear you."

"I just wanted to congratulate you on making the play," Meg said.

"Thanks." Elizabeth thought that she wanted to say something else but was hesitant to do so. After an uncomfortable silence, Elizabeth said, "Well, the bell is going to ring, so I'd better sit down."

"Yeah, me too," she said, but Elizabeth had already turned away. "Oh, boy. Warning her about Brad is going to be much harder than I thought," she muttered to herself as she took her seat.

Once English class began, Elizabeth didn't have a chance to think about anything other than *The Great Gatsby*. The class had spent over a month reading, discussing, and analyzing the novel by F. Scott Fitzgerald, and today they spent the entire period on an essay test. When the school day ended, things became even more hectic. First, she went to tennis practice. Practices were becoming very intense as the team worked hard to maintain their number-one ranking. After tennis, she hurried to play practice. She was a little late, but Miss Johnson, the director, didn't mind since she was coming from another school activity. Because this was the first night of rehearsals, they spent the time on introductions and explanations about the type of play, its length and the nature of rehearsals, and the performance dates. Thus, Elizabeth didn't get a chance to test her acting skills. She was anxious to see if Brad was right that she got the part only because the director was desperate.

When Elizabeth got home that night, she was absolutely exhausted. With only a few words to her parents, she went upstairs and shut her door. She knew that she should work on her homework, but she had to talk to Brad first. She picked up her phone and called him. When Brad answered, she smiled.

"Hey, Brad! How's it going?"

"Elizabeth, why are you whispering?"

"Because I don't want my parents to hear me. They think I'm doing homework. Remember, I told you that they were really mad that I came home after curfew Saturday night. I'm not supposed to talk to you on the phone or text you for a week. They wanted to take my phone away, but I lied and convinced them that I needed it to text some people for a group project."

"That's really dumb. How can you stand your parents?"

"I'm beginning to wonder about that myself, but I'm not letting them get to me. After all, I'm talking to you right now, aren't I?"

"Yeah, and I'm glad, too. I missed seeing you after tennis tonight. How did things go today?"

Despite the fact that she wasn't supposed to be on the phone, they continued to talk for forty-five minutes. Their conversation was going so well that Elizabeth hated to tell him about her rehearsal schedule. "I've got play practice again tomorrow, Wednesday, and Thursday."

"That sucks, Elizabeth. I hate this. I'm going to miss you so much." He didn't sound angry this time; he just sounded disappointed.

"I know. I'll miss you, too. I really like it when you drive me home after tennis, but we can do that again on Friday. We don't have rehearsal on Friday. I do have tennis, but you have football anyway."

"Actually, I don't. We're practicing on Saturday morning instead. Coach doesn't want to tire us out by having too many practices before the playoff game on Saturday night. It's going to be strange not having football on Friday."

"Well, at least we both have more relaxed schedules this Friday; we'll have more time together on Friday night. I'd better go now; I should study for physics, but we've been talking for about forty-five minutes and I'm too tired now. I think I'll just go to bed."

"Good idea. I'm glad you made the right choice and talked to me instead of studying. Good night. I love you."

Her heart soared when she hung up the phone. Once again, she felt like the luckiest girl in the world to have Brad Evans as a boyfriend. Every time he told her he loved her, she felt tingly all over. Shoving aside her unopened backpack with her homework inside, she danced around her room as she got ready for bed. As she sailed into her bed and snuggled under the covers, she smiled and thought that Friday night couldn't possibly come quickly enough.

CHAPTER 12

It turned out that Friday came quickly. Elizabeth was so busy that the week whizzed past. It seemed to her that she hung up the phone after talking to Brad on Monday night, blinked, and it was already Friday.

When she arrived at school that morning, she found him waiting at her locker as usual. He smiled at her, and when she reached him, he bent down and gave her a kiss. "Morning, Liz. It's finally Friday!"

"Thank goodness! I can't wait until tennis practice is over. We're preparing for tomorrow's meet so practice might be a bit longer, but we'll be done by seven. And I don't have play rehearsal, remember, so at seven the evening is ours!"

Brad grinned at her slyly. "I have a great idea," he said excitedly. "Why don't you skip tennis and we could drive to Oak Heights? We can eat at a fancy restaurant and go to a movie. I know it's almost two hours away, but if we leave right after school we could make it there and still be back reasonably close to your curfew. What do you think?"

"I think it sounds great, but..." Elizabeth trailed off.

"What do you mean, 'but'?" His forehead creased, which told Elizabeth that he was growing angry. She was used to that look by now, and it made her nervous.

"Nothing. I would really love to go to Oak Heights with you; it sounds so romantic. It's just that I'm afraid to skip tennis. It's an important practice, since we have a big meet tomorrow. No varsity player has skipped out on a practice this year. Coach Thompson will be furious."

Brad sighed heavily. "Well, jeez, Elizabeth. Who's more important to you: me, or Coach Thompson? It seems to me that the stupid tennis team means more to you than our relationship. If that's your attitude, then fine. Go to your dumb practice. And here I was trying to work around that ridiculous curfew of yours, but I guess you want to satisfy everyone but me. Thanks a lot." He kicked her locker hard enough to dent it and cause several heads to turn their way, and then he stomped off.

"Brad, wait!" she called, rushing forward to grab his arm. "Of course you're the most important to me. You're the best part of my life—you should know that. I was just caught off guard, that's all. I'd much rather spend the evening with you than with Thompson and the team. Let's do it!"

With that, Brad let out a whoop and grabbed her around her waist, encircling her in a huge bear hug. That was one of the things Elizabeth loved about Brad: even though he was quick to anger, he was also quick to come around again. When he did, he was always happy and made her feel so good. She had once read a magazine article that said fighting was okay because then you got to make up. She now understood what that meant and agreed whole-heartedly. She hugged him back. When he didn't let go for what seemed like more than a minute, Elizabeth noticed that people were giving them weird looks. She informed him, "Brad, we're in the middle of the hallway and people are everywhere. They're starting to stare."

"Then let them stare," he said without letting go. "Remember, I warned you that people would be jealous of what we have. Let's not let their envy get to us." He gave her one last extra tight squeeze, leaned back, planted a kiss on her lips, and then let her go. "Besides, I'm Brad Evans. If anyone is staring, they're just in awe of me and jealous of you. Come on. I'll walk you to trig."

Elizabeth groaned. "Oh, please don't mention trig. I haven't done my homework all week. I don't have anything to hand in today, and I know I'm going to do poorly on the quiz we're having."

"Well, math is probably just too hard for you, Liz. Maybe you should rethink your career choice; I don't think engineering is for you."

"I really do want to be an engineer, but it sure has been hard to keep up with my classes these days."

"Liz, I love you, but I don't think you're smart enough for these tough classes."

She sighed. "I don't know. Maybe you're right." She didn't think that the only reason she was falling behind was that she spent every evening on the phone with Brad instead of doing her homework.

"Don't think about that now, Liz. Just think about tonight and how much fun we're going to have. See you later!"

━━━

Elizabeth clutched her tennis racket hard as she walked to the tennis courts early Saturday morning. It was a gray, overcast day. The clouds seemed to hang very low in the sky, and she thought they looked heavy. A brisk, cold wind whipped strands of hair out of her ponytail and into her face. She didn't bother to push them away. Brown leaves crunched beneath her feet as she walked, and one stuck in her sock and poked her ankle. She left that alone, too.

As she walked, she thought about last night. Just as they planned, Elizabeth and Brad had left for Oak Heights right after school. Not once during the entire evening did she regret skipping tennis; Brad had been relaxed and happy the entire evening. They had talked a great deal about everything under the sun. Sometimes they talked about funny things, and they both laughed until their sides hurt. Other times they talked about very serious things, and each one listened intently to the other. Brad had willingly used some of his dad's allowance to treat her to a nice dinner and a movie. After the movie, they had talked all the way home, never running out of things to say to each other.

They had arrived home an hour past Elizabeth's curfew, and when Brad pulled into her driveway, she had noticed immediately that all the lights were on in the house. Her parents had been waiting up for her. She didn't care, though, and had taken her time kissing Brad good night in the moonlight.

Her parents had been furious when she entered the house. They began to lecture her, but she had cut them off, telling them that they were way too controlling. She had taken Brad's advice and informed them that she was practically an adult and could do as she pleased, and then she had marched up the stairs to her room and slammed the door. She had expected them to follow her up and continue berating her, but they hadn't. She had tossed and turned all night wondering why they had left her alone.

In the morning, they told her that she was grounded for one month, and in that time she was not allowed to associate with Brad outside of school. She was not to see him, catch a ride with him, or talk to him on the phone. After a month had passed, they would reevaluate the situation and perhaps allow her to see him again.

Brad was so right about my parents, she thought as she walked to tennis on that cold Saturday morning. *They are so overpowering. I wonder why I never noticed it before. Brad warned me that they would try to keep us apart. He was right. I can't believe Mom and Dad would do that to me. They can say anything they want, though, but they can't actually keep us apart. I don't have to listen to them. They'll just get angrier and angrier, but they can't really do anything to keep me from seeing Brad.*

At last she reached the courts. *Great,* she thought as she noticed that the team had already begun to warm up. *My parents' little chat made me late. Now Thompson will have one more thing to get after me about. I wonder what he'll say about my skipping out last night. Whatever happens, I don't really care. It was worth it!*

"Carter! Nice of you to grace the team with your presence." Coach Thompson's voice was filled with fury as he greeted Elizabeth at the entrance to the courts. "Just where do you think you were yesterday?"

Elizabeth looked down at the ground. She had tried to convince herself that she was glad she skipped practice, but upon seeing her teammates playing the game she loved, she realized she felt awful about it. She did have fun with Brad, but she regretted that she had abandoned the team. "Something unexpected came up; I couldn't make it. I'm sorry."

"So am I, Elizabeth. I am very disappointed in you. I hate to do this because we really need you, but you can't play in the meet today."

"What?" she gasped.

"You can't just skip a practice and expect to play in the next meet. I'm sorry, but you're not playing today." With that, Coach Thompson turned and went back to the rest of the team.

Tears immediately sprang to her eyes. She began to walk toward the bleachers, but something caught her eye. Turning back toward the street, she saw Brad's car pulling into the parking lot. She jogged toward him.

"Oh, Brad," she lamented when she reached his car. "The coach won't let me play today."

"I thought he might pull something like that, so I came to get you. Come on, let's get out of here."

"I can't. Just because I can't play doesn't mean I can leave. I'm expected to stay and cheer on the rest of the team."

"Why? What has that team done for you?"

"It's a team, Brad, and I'm part of it. You should know from football, basketball, and track how that stuff works."

"Yeah, but those are real sports. Tennis is just dumb. It doesn't really matter, so why stick around? Now come on; I've got to get to my practice. Who would you rather support today, me or Thompson and his bimbos?"

"You, of course, but—"

"No buts, Elizabeth. In fact, I don't think you need Thompson's hassle anymore. Go down there right now and tell him that you quit."

"But I don't want to quit!"

His face turned red. "I said go quit, Elizabeth. I'm tired of you wasting so much time with this pretend sport. Now if you want to keep going out with me, go quit! You owe it to me after all the money I spent on you last night." He shoved her back toward the courts, causing her to lose her balance and fall to the ground, scraping her palms and skinning one knee.

"Brad! Ouch!" She climbed to her feet and brushed off her tennis skirt. She glanced back at Brad, who was standing against his car, his arms folded tightly across his chest. His face was twisted into that all too familiar scowl.

"That's what happens when you're so clumsy. Suck it up and get going."

Clutching her racket against her chest and fiddling with the strings, she walked back onto the courts. She felt sick. She loved the team and didn't want to quit, but she loved Brad, too. She knew that for him and for their relationship, she had to do it. Slowly, she approached her coach as he stood along the fence at the back of the courts.

"What is it, Elizabeth?" Thompson asked as he noticed Elizabeth standing at his side. "You're supposed to be on the bleachers. Hey. You're bleeding. What happened?"

"Nothing. I just tripped. Look, I'm really sorry, but I quit the team." Before he could respond, she turned and ran off the courts. She hopped into Brad's car, and he squealed out of the parking lot. When she looked out her window, she saw her former coach staring after her, his clipboard at his side. She couldn't see the expression on his face, for her eyes were filled with tears.

CHAPTER 13

Elizabeth sat cross-legged on her bed and stared at the books spread around her. She had so much to do that she didn't even know where to begin. She had homework in every single subject this weekend, and she really wasn't looking forward to any of it. Homework never used to bother her before. School had always been easy for her, and she had fun learning new things, but her classes seemed much more difficult this year. True, she was in a number of advanced classes, but they were subjects that were supposed to interest her. Admittedly, the subjects she once loved—especially trigonometry and physics—were starting to become burdensome. She was beginning to think that Brad was right; maybe she just wasn't cut out for classes like this. She hated to admit that, since it probably meant that she wasn't cut out for engineering, either.

She sighed and picked up her trig book. *Oh well. I might as well start somewhere, and this is the class I'm the farthest behind in.* After staring at the first problem for a few minutes, she shut her book and looked around her room. Doing so upset her even more, for all around her room were reminders of tennis: pictures of her with her teammates, newspaper articles about the team, ribbons and trophies she had won over the years at various events, and the varsity letter jacket her mom and dad had bought her earlier in the fall when she first told them she had made the varsity team. Her parents had wanted her to have the jacket so she had a place to proudly display her varsity letter when she earned it at the end of the season. Tears stung her eyes as she realized that would never happen. She had quit the team yesterday. She couldn't play in any more meets. She couldn't help the team win the state tournament. She wouldn't earn the varsity letter.

Suddenly, she couldn't stand the sight of all of her tennis stuff. Jumping off her bed, she began to rip everything down. She tore her pictures and ribbons off her walls and yanked her trophies off their shelves. She jerked her jacket off its hanger and whipped some stray tennis balls off the floor. Bundling everything together, she shoved the works under the bed.

Just as she was standing up, she heard the doorbell ring. Her heart began to beat quickly in her chest; maybe it was Brad. Her parents were still angry about her coming in way past curfew last night, and they probably would not be happy about Brad coming to the house since she wasn't supposed to see him for a month, but she didn't care. She was thrilled that he would drop in to see her. Giving the bundle of tennis things a final kick under the bed and wiping her eyes, she ran out of her room.

She stopped short at the top of the stairs, however, when she heard voices. Her mom had answered the door and wasn't talking to Brad. She was talking to Meg! What in the world was *she* doing here? Elizabeth definitely did not want to see Meg. She turned and tiptoed quickly back to her room. She threw herself onto the bed and picked up her nearest textbook, figuring that if she seemed engrossed in homework, Meg would go away.

Downstairs, Meg was not going away. "It's good to see you, too, Mrs. Carter," she said.

"Please come in, Meg. Why haven't we seen you around more lately?"

She hesitated. "I don't know. Elizabeth and I have both been too busy, I guess."

"Well, I'm glad you're here today. Lizzie is in her room doing homework, but I'm sure she wouldn't mind having a break. Go up and see her."

"I will. Thanks, Mrs. Carter." Meg walked slowly up the steps and knocked on Elizabeth's door.

Inside the room, Elizabeth froze. Meg was outside her door! She sat on her bed for a moment, silent and unmoving. Then, pretending that she didn't know it was Meg outside her door, she called, "I'm really busy, Mom. Could you come back in awhile? I'm right in the middle of a physics problem."

"Um, Elizabeth? It's me, Meg. I'd like to talk to you. Could I come in for awhile?"

Elizabeth sat up straight and pushed her hair out of her face. Now what was she supposed to do? She did not want to talk to Meg, but she couldn't exactly refuse to let her in. *Oh, don't be ridiculous,* she told herself, annoyed. *This is Meg, not a monster. Sure, we may have grown apart, but there's no reason to be nervous about seeing her. Brad wouldn't like it, though. I'll just keep the conversation brief and she'll leave.*

She shuffled across the room, opened her door a crack, and peeked into the hallway. "Meg, what are you doing here?" She didn't want to be too welcoming, but she didn't want to sound too mean, either, so she tried to keep her voice neutral.

"Well, we really haven't talked or anything in awhile, and I guess I just wanted to see how things were going with you."

"I've got tons of homework and I should work on my lines for the play, but I guess I could take a *short* break."

She walked back to her bed and sat uncomfortably on the end. She noticed that rather than flopping down beside her or stretching out on the floor as she would have in the past, Meg leaned against the wall opposite the bed.

Looking at the bare walls and frowning, she got right to the point. "Elizabeth, why did you quit the tennis team yesterday?"

Elizabeth sighed. "Look, I just did, okay?"

"Come on, Liz. It's me, Meg. I know how much you love tennis. Why'd you quit?"

To get Meg to drop the subject, she tried the old joke they had shared for so long. "I noticed that Coach Thompson only had eyes for you. When I realized that I didn't have a chance with him, I figured that I might as well quit."

It didn't work; they weren't on joking terms anymore. "Elizabeth, be serious."

She shrugged. "I just got sick and tired of Thompson's control over my life. If he had his way, the team would be the only thing in my life, but that's hardly realistic. I've got these hard classes, the play, and I'd like to have time for my boyfriend. I'm not willing to sacrifice everything to please Thompson. Tennis really isn't that important." She avoided looking directly at Meg.

"When did you decide that?"

"I've been feeling it for a long time—even last season I was getting sick of it."

Meg took her hands out of her pockets and crossed her arms over her stomach. "That's funny. You never mentioned anything to me about that."

"What's your point? There are a lot of things I didn't share with you," she lied. She was beginning to feel very uncomfortable with this conversation; she was afraid she knew where Meg was going. Brad had warned her that Meg would try to come between them, and she didn't want to let that happen. She was desperate to end their talk and make Meg leave, even if it meant hurting her.

"Oh," Meg said quietly, looking down at the floor. The room was quiet for a few moments. Then Meg began again. "How's Brad?"

"Great. Why?"

"Just wondering. I've been wanting to hear stories about you and the great Brad Evans, but I never see you anymore. You're always with him."

"That's because he's great to be with."

"Really?" Meg's tone was cold.

Elizabeth stood up and leaned into the corner at the head of her bed, putting more space and the entire bed between her and Meg. "Yes. What are you getting at, Meg?" Her tone was defensive.

Meg sighed and ran her hands through her short hair, and Elizabeth realized she'd had a haircut. Even though she saw her every day, she really hadn't paid that much attention to her. She didn't mention that she liked it; Meg interrupted her thoughts.

"Elizabeth." Meg sighed again. "I really didn't want things to go this way today. I didn't want to get into this right away, but I can't help it. I've gotta do it. Elizabeth, Brad Evans is a jerk. You've got to get away from him. He—"

Elizabeth interrupted her. "Oh, really? And since when are you such an expert on my boyfriend? You don't even know him. He won't have anything to do with you; the most he's ever said to you is 'hi'. Tell me how you know him so well based on that." Her heart was pounding. Her ears were burning and she knew that they were bright red. She could hardly contain her anger. It was hard to keep from shouting at Meg, but she didn't want her parents to hear the conversation and butt in.

Meg didn't seem bothered by Elizabeth's reaction. She continued, undaunted. "For starters, there's the fact that he won't have anything to do with me. Maybe he thinks he's better than some people. That sounds like a jerk to me."

"So that's it! I knew you were jealous, Meg. Look, you're not the center of everyone's world. You need to get over yourself."

Meg ignored the angry tirade. "Listen to me, Lizzie—Brad is controlling you. Why did you quit the tennis team yesterday? Was it your choice, or did Brad make you do it?" Without giving her a chance to answer, Meg rushed on. "And who do you hang around with besides Brad? What about all those clubs you wanted to join? How does he treat you when you're together? I'll bet—"

Elizabeth couldn't listen any longer. "Brad was right! He warned me about you. He said you'd try to break us up, but I didn't think you'd stoop that low. I thought you'd be happy for me that I've found such a great guy, but apparently I was wrong about you, Meg. You just can't handle the fact that I have an amazing boyfriend—the hottest guy in school—can you? Of course I spend all my time with him! He's great to be with. We have fun, he's sweet, and we love each other. He was glad when I quit the team, but that's because he cares about me so much that he wants to spend as much time with me as he can. But you wouldn't understand, would you? You've never had a real boyfriend.

You're so desperate for a relationship that you fantasize about the tennis coach." That was a low blow, and Elizabeth knew it, but she didn't care. Meg deserved it.

"You can't fool me, Meg," she continued, her voice rising. "I saw you talking with Sarah Wilson at lunch awhile ago. You don't think Brad and I knew what you were up to? It's so obvious. You're both jealous of what we have and you want to break us up. How pathetic.

"Brad and I love each other, and he is not a jerk. How dare you say that! He cares about me and he needs me. You have no idea what is going on in his life right now. He needs me to be there for him. You don't understand what we have."

"Elizabeth, please listen—"

"No, Meg, I won't listen. I don't want to listen to the angry, jealous accusations of an ex-friend. Get out."

"Lizzie—"

"Now." When Meg didn't budge, Elizabeth said, "I don't want to talk to you again. I don't need your jealousy. Leave." She turned away and sat back down on her bed, her back to Meg. She sat unmoving for several long seconds. Finally, she heard Meg move toward the door.

Elizabeth heard Meg turn the knob and then stop. "Lizzie," she said softly, "I'm not jealous. I'm scared for you. Please don't let Brad take you over. I want to help you. Please talk to me when you're ready." Before Elizabeth could respond, she slipped out of the room and shut the door.

Elizabeth sat very still for a long time after Meg had gone. When she finally moved, it was to pick up her phone. She was so appalled by what Meg had said that she felt sick. The only person she wanted to talk to right now was Brad. She needed to tell him that she loved him, and she wanted to make plans to see him again soon. She would have to sneak around to do it, but she didn't care.

With shaky fingers, she dialed Brad's number. The call went right to his voicemail. Desperate to talk to him, she called his home phone. A woman answered, probably his mother, Elizabeth thought, though she had never met her. When she asked to speak with Brad, the woman replied that he was out with friends and that she didn't know when he would return. Disappointed, Elizabeth hung up the phone.

She stared at her books, but she definitely wasn't in the mood for homework. She stuffed everything back into her backpack unfinished. She would just have to turn in incomplete work tomorrow. She didn't want to practice her lines for the play, either, so the script went into her backpack, too. Her relationship with Brad was the only thing in her life that she cared about right now.

She looked around her room sadly and realized that Brad was right. Everyone and everything in the world was trying to work against them, but she couldn't understand why. She took out some paper and began to write a long love letter to her boyfriend. It didn't occur to her that as she sat alone in her room, freshly stripped of all her beloved tennis mementos, her boyfriend was out enjoying himself with a bunch of his friends.

CHAPTER 14

Elizabeth stood under a streetlight and leaned her head back against the cold metal post. Talking a deep breath, she closed her eyes. What a horrible Monday this had been! She had felt completely lost in trigonometry. She was so far behind in her work that she could barely even follow Mr. Charlton's explanations anymore. To her dismay, he had announced that there would be a very big test this Thursday, and she was sure to fail. Currently, she was barely squeaking by with a C-, but failing Thursday's test would surely lower her grade to a D. After trig, her classes hadn't gotten any better. She had done poorly on the pop quiz given in American History, and she'd had to tell her English teacher that her paper wasn't ready.

At least she'd had the opportunity to finish her paper after school. Immediately after the final bell, Elizabeth had felt empty and lonely inside. Standing at her locker, she watched people rush out of the building. Some were hurrying to after-school jobs, and others had club meetings. She saw some of her former teammates head toward the courts, and others just wanted to leave after a long day. Even Brad had left right at three thirty for football practice. Elizabeth had felt as if she were the only person in the world with nowhere to go, but then she had realized that for the first time in a long time, she had some spare time on her hands. She had an hour and a half before play practice. Thinking that she could get some work done, she went to the computer lab to finish her English paper.

She'd felt good about herself after finishing the paper, until she had gone to play practice. It was quickly becoming evident that acting was not her strong suit. Because she didn't devote time at home to her script, she had difficulty remembering her lines and relied on the script much more than the other actors. She constantly had to peer at the script and was not interacting with the other characters the way she should, and she was having trouble with the blocking. She just couldn't get it right—she was always standing in the wrong spot and moving in the wrong direction. After rehearsal that night, Miss Johnson had pulled her aside and told her that she really needed to work harder at the play. She had explained that acting took a lot of hard work and that Elizabeth needed to spend time outside the rehearsals learning her lines.

Leaning against the streetlight in the school parking lot, Elizabeth grew angry again just thinking of that conversation. Did Miss Johnson think she was stupid? She knew that acting was hard work! It was not that she didn't want to spend time on the play; it was almost impossible for her to find the time. Between spending time with Brad, talking to him on the phone each night, and trying to work on her many difficult subjects, it was hard to make time for the play. *Thank goodness I don't have to deal with tennis anymore!* she thought with a huff.

As she was stewing, she saw a car drive into the parking lot. She grabbed her backpack and stood up straight. Holding her bag, she waited for her dad to pull up. When the car stopped in front of her, though, she was surprised to find that it was Brad. Elizabeth grinned and ran over to the car.

"Brad, what are you doing here? It's great to see you!"

"The handsome prince rode in to give his princess a ride home. Hop in." He grinned back at her.

"Oh, Brad, I can't. My father is coming to pick me up, and he'd kill me if I left before he got here."

Brad shot her one of his crooked smiles that she thought was so cute. "He's not coming. He said I could come and get you." When Elizabeth just stood there and stared at him, Brad asked, "Well, are you going to get in or just stand out there in the cold all night?"

"You have got to be kidding. There is no way my father would agree to that, especially since I'm not supposed to see you outside of school for a month."

"He did, I promise."

"Brad. Really."

"Check your phone. I bet he sent you a text."

She pulled her phone out of her pocket and glanced at the screen. "You're right! How in the world did you get him to let you come get me?" Elizabeth was still standing outside Brad's car.

"It was pretty easy, actually. I just went to your house and charmed your parents. I told them how sorry I was for getting you home late. I explained that when I'm with you, the time just goes so fast that I lose track of it. That's true, you know." He winked at her, and she felt her stomach flutter.

"Anyway, they said it was okay for me to come after I told them you had a really bad day and I wanted to give you this." He held up a soft and fuzzy light brown teddy bear with a red rose rubber-banded onto its wrist. "I hope this makes up for your bad day," he said softly.

At that, Elizabeth leaped into the car. "Oh, Brad, you are the sweetest boyfriend in the world! Thank you so much! You always make everything seem all right." Hugging the bear with one arm, she put her other arm around Brad's neck and kissed him.

After a few moments, Brad straightened up and said solemnly, "As much as I don't want to, I have to take you home. I promised you parents that I would just pick you up and bring you straight home—it's the only way they would agree. If we get you home right away, maybe they'll change their minds about us not seeing each other outside of school for a month."

"I hope so. That's really a pain, but I wouldn't let them stop me from seeing you, you know."

"I know," he replied, "and that means a lot to me, Liz."

"Thank you so much for the bear and the rose, Brad. I really needed something to cheer me up. Rehearsal was awful." She proceeded to tell him everything that had happened, including the talk she'd had with the director. "I can't believe her comments! She was actually insinuating that I'm not cut out for the play."

Brad looked over at her. "Well, maybe she's right. I've heard you do your lines. Elizabeth, I love you, but I really don't think acting is your thing."

"Thanks a lot. Your support means so much to me," she said sarcastically.

"Hey, I do support you. If I didn't, would I have gone through the trouble of asking your parents' permission to pick you up, and then drive all the way over to the school to get you? And would I have given you a teddy bear and a rose?"

Elizabeth gave her bear a little squeeze and rubbed its soft fur against her cheek. "No, I guess not."

"I just hate to see you put yourself through this when you're not any good. And besides, look at how much of your time it's taking. It's taking away from us. Why would you want to spend your time struggling with something you can't do when you could be having fun with me?"

"What are you suggesting?"

"I'm really not suggesting anything, but to me, it would make sense for you to quit the play. It's not worth your hassle."

"Brad, I can't quit. That wouldn't be fair to the other actors. They'd have to find someone else, and doing so would interfere with their rehearsals. The performance is scheduled, and it's just over a month away."

"You'd be doing them a favor, Elizabeth. They could find someone better. You'd be doing yourself a favor, too. And you'd be doing me a favor." He took one hand off the steering wheel and placed it on her leg.

"I don't know..."

Removing his hand and holding the steering wheel again, Brad continued. "You've just got to accept the fact that you're bad at some things, Liz. You were bad at tennis, and now you're not on the team. You—"

Elizabeth interrupted him. "I was not bad at tennis! I was on the varsity team, but I quit."

"Yeah, but do you think that if you were any good Thompson would have let you quit? He would have fought to make you stay, but he didn't. He just let you walk away. Coaches don't let good players just walk off like that, Liz."

"I really hadn't thought of it that way."

"Well, it's true. And tennis wasn't your only problem. You were a bad friend, and now Meg has abandoned you. Even Jenny, the one who follows people around, doesn't hang around you anymore. You're a bad actress; you said yourself that the director suggested that you're not cut out for the play. And now you're being a bad girlfriend. I love you so much, Liz. Don't you want to please me by quitting so we can be together more?"

They rode in silence as they approached her house. Confused, Elizabeth contemplated what he had said. She didn't think any of it was true, but she couldn't deny it, either. The more she thought, the more she believed what he said.

Brad pulled into her driveway. "Just think about it, okay? You don't have to be a bad girlfriend. All I'm asking you to do is quit the play. I'd like to be able to spend more time with you." He stared down at his lap and spoke quietly. "Everything else in my life sucks. I enjoy football, but that's almost over. I've been scouted out by several colleges, but I won't know anything for a while, so I'm all tense about that. Sure, basketball will be starting up soon, but that doesn't bring me pleasure like football does. I don't have a family; my dad and brother walked out on me, and my mom doesn't seem to want me around. I seem to be a burden for her. She's hardly ever home, probably because she's either working to support me or is trying to get away from me. You're the only person I have who is close to me, so I want to be around you as much as I can. The play is just something that keeps us apart." He looked up at her, then leaned over and hugged her. "You'd better go inside. I don't want your parents to think I kept you out too long. Good night, Liz. I love you."

Elizabeth opened the car door but paused before climbing out. "I love you, too, Brad. I'll think about the play." She stepped out of the car and shut the door. As she watched Brad back out and drive away, she absentmindedly rubbed the teddy bear's head. Then she walked slowly into her house.

The following evening, Elizabeth was nervous as she walked into the auditorium. She had tried to study her lines the night before but had fallen asleep while doing so. Consequently, she was unprepared for tonight's rehearsal. To add to her worries, Brad's comments kept running through her mind. He had tried again today to convince her to quit. He had seemed irritated that she didn't promise to quit, but she just couldn't—not yet, anyway. She'd see how tonight's rehearsal went.

Unfortunately, it didn't go any better than the night before. If anything, it seemed even worse. She was so afraid of performing poorly that she made more mistakes than ever. To make matters worse, she noticed Brad slip into the auditorium and sit down about half way through the rehearsal. Why was he there? Did he want to see if she was good after all? Was he checking to see if she was going to quit? She was so distracted by his presence that she couldn't even get her lines right when she read them from the script. She was relieved when rehearsal was finally over.

She gathered up her things and was about to find Brad when Miss Johnson approached her. "Elizabeth," she began, placing her hand on her shoulder, "what's wrong? You seem very distraught."

"I'm so sorry about tonight's rehearsal, Miss Johnson. It won't happen again, I promise. I will get better."

"I'm sure you will." Miss Johnson studied her for a moment. "Would you like to talk about what's bothering you?" she asked gently. "I'm a good listener."

Before she could reply, Brad appeared at Elizabeth's side. He took hold of her arm and said, "I'm sorry to interrupt, but your dad sent me to get you, Elizabeth. We'd better leave."

"I won't keep you, Elizabeth. See you tomorrow." Miss Johnson left her and went backstage.

When the director had gone, Brad tightened his grip on Elizabeth's arm and grumbled, "Come on. Let's go." He marched her up the aisle and out of the auditorium. Kicking open the front door to the school, he pulled Elizabeth into the parking lot. He said nothing until they were both inside his car, and then he exploded.

"You didn't quit!" he shouted.

"I thought about it. I really did."

"Then what was that crap you told Johnson about how you'll get better? That didn't sound to me like you're thinking about quitting. What are you trying to pull, Elizabeth?"

"Nothing! It's just—"

"Forget it! I don't want to hear it!" Brad hadn't lowered his voice, and his shouting hurt her ears. "Apparently you don't care that much about me. You'd rather please the drama director than me. 'Oh, I'm so sorry that I suck, Miss Johnson. Please forgive me. I'll give up my whole life and work hard so I can pretend to be good at something I'm not.'" He sneered and mocked Elizabeth's voice.

"Cut it out, Brad."

"You don't have the right to tell me what to do, Elizabeth. I can't believe that you didn't quit. Some girlfriend you're turning out to be. I was better off with Sarah."

"Brad, please don't be angry!" Her voice shook as she tried not to cry.

"Tell me why I shouldn't be mad, Elizabeth." His voice was filled with fury. "You were supposed to quit tonight!" On the last word, he reached over and smacked her across the face.

Tears instantly sprang to Elizabeth's eyes and ran down her cheeks. Her hands flew up to her injured cheek. It was fiery hot and stung horribly from the blow. She was in such pain, both physically and emotionally, that she couldn't even speak. As she sat there holding her cheek, her entire body began to shake. She couldn't stop her tremors, and she couldn't stop the tears from coming, either.

Without a word, Brad started the car and headed for Elizabeth's house. Upon reaching their driveway, he said only two things. First, "You'd better pull yourself together before your parents see you like that." Then, "Think hard about what means more to you—our relationship or that stupid play."

Unable to speak, Elizabeth got out of the car, and Brad drove away.

CHAPTER 15

J ust before lunch the next day, a note from the office was delivered to Elizabeth in class. It said that she should come to the office because she had a delivery. Curious, she headed straight there as soon as the bell rang. She approached Mrs. Keaton, the secretary, and explained why she was there.

"Oh, Elizabeth!" exclaimed the secretary. "Are you a lucky girl! Look what came for you." She pointed to a table behind her desk. Sitting on the table was a huge vase filled with what looked like a dozen red, pink, white, and yellow roses. Attached to the vase was another teddy bear.

"Wow! That's for me?" Elizabeth couldn't believe it.

"It sure is," came a deep voice behind her.

She spun around and found Brad standing behind her, looking down at her with a very serious and loving expression in his eyes.

"You sent these?" the secretary asked Brad.

"Yes, ma'am."

"Young lady," Mrs. Keaton addressed Elizabeth, "you have one terrific boyfriend. Make sure you hang on to him!"

Elizabeth reached back and gave Brad a squeeze. "Just a second, Brad. I'll grab my flowers and then we'll go to lunch."

"You should keep them in here until after school, dear," stated the secretary. "What a nice couple," she said to herself as they left the office.

As they headed toward the cafeteria, Elizabeth and Brad spoke at the same time.

"Brad, I'm sorry..."

"Elizabeth, I'm so sorry..."

They both laughed.

"Liz," he began again, "please, please forgive me. I shouldn't have hit you. I am so sorry." He gently rubbed her cheek. "Oh, no, I even bruised you. I don't deserve to have you. No wonder you don't want to give up the play. I'm such a jerk." His eyes filled with tears.

"Oh, Brad, I'm sorry, too. I should have quit the play yesterday. I thought about it all night. You were right; I'm bad at acting, and I shouldn't keep making myself miserable. Besides, I'd much rather spend my time with you."

"Liz, it feels so good to hear you say that."

"I'll quit tonight, I promise." When she smiled up at him, she felt the bruise and she winced..

"I really hurt you. I truly am sorry, Liz. Did your parents notice?"

"Sort of, but I went right upstairs when I got home so they didn't see it then. This morning I skipped breakfast. As I was leaving the house, my mom asked me if there was something wrong with my face. I told her we had a lab in physics yesterday and I goofed up, causing a little explosion. I think she bought it."

They began to talk about parents then, and they both shared frustrations with each other until the bell signaled the end of the lunch period. Brad gave her a hug before he went to class. "I'll see you this evening. I'll sit in the auditorium during rehearsal for moral support. Good luck!"

———

That evening, Elizabeth didn't know whether she was relieved or apprehensive that Brad was in the auditorium, but she was definitely uptight about quitting. She wanted to do well at rehearsal anyway, just to prove to herself that she wasn't that bad. She also knew that Brad would be watching her every move and waiting for her to quit. She didn't know when or how she was going to quit, and that made her even more nervous.

Her uneasiness showed throughout the rehearsal, causing her to make many mistakes. Finally, Miss Johnson told everyone to take a break, and she approached Elizabeth and pulled her aside.

"Elizabeth, I have some bad news for you. I'm very sorry to have to do this, but I have to replace you. Each day we are getting closer to our performance, but I don't see you improving. I can't give you any more chances; we don't have time. I have to reassign the part now before it's too late for anyone new to learn lines. I'm sorry that it didn't work out, Elizabeth." With that, she left to talk to another actor about his lines.

Elizabeth was dumbfounded. She knew that she was having some problems, but she never dreamed that she would be kicked out of the play. *Brad was right—I am terrible. I can't do anything. Miss Johnson just told me that I'm worthless. I'm so bad that she'd rather give the part to someone new even though we're well into our rehearsal schedule. I didn't want to admit it to myself before, but Brad was right about everything else, too. I must have been a bad tennis player, or Coach Thompson would have tried to convince me to stay on the team. He must be glad I'm gone. I'm also doing horribly in my classes; maybe I'm not smart enough to be an engineer. And no one wants to be friends with me. I'm just lucky I have Brad. Without him, where would I be? I wouldn't have anyone.*

Sadly, Elizabeth left the stage, gathered her things, and walked up the aisle toward Brad. She clutched the flowers and bear he had sent her that day. "Let's go," she said quietly as she continued to walk toward the door.

"Jeez, it took you long enough," he complained. "I was hoping that you'd quit right away."

Elizabeth said nothing as she walked out of the school and into the parking lot, her head hanging low. She stopped when Brad tugged gently on her arm.

"Hey, Liz? What's wrong? Aren't you glad to be done with that?"

"The director kicked me out of the play, Brad." Elizabeth sniffled. "She said that I wasn't cut out for acting."

"Well, that's great! That way you didn't have to quit."

"I can't believe I was so bad that she didn't want me to be part of the cast."

Brad shoved his hands into his pockets and glared at her. "Well, really, Elizabeth, I don't see what the problem is. You were going to quit anyway. So she kicked you off; what's the difference?"

"Nothing, I guess," she mumbled.

"Look, I told you a long time ago that acting wasn't your thing. If you had listened to me then, you wouldn't be having this problem now, would you?" He sounded quite annoyed. "You're just being stupid, Elizabeth. You're lucky I'm willing to put up with you. No one else wants you. If you didn't have me, you'd be totally alone. Now get in the car. I'd better take you home before your parents go ballistic again."

———

Things did not get better for Elizabeth the next day. It was Thursday, the day of her big trig test. Brad and the play had consumed so much of her time and energy that week that she was not prepared to take it. She did her best, but she had a very bad feeling that she didn't pass.

Between classes, she noticed new signs for the tennis team posted all over the hallways. The team had finished the season in first place, and the players were on their way to the state tournament. One of the posters listed all of the varsity players, and a wave of sadness washed over her. Her name was not on the list. As she stared at the poster, something caught her eye. Meg was listed as a varsity player; she had moved up when Elizabeth quit. *Good for Meg,* she thought somberly. *Even though we're not friends anymore, I am happy for her. I bet her parents were thrilled. I wonder how things are going with her science classes. Are her mom and dad still pushing her to be a doctor? I'll never know, I guess.*

I am glad to see that Meg is on the varsity team; she needs something. She doesn't have a boyfriend. I am so glad to have Brad. It's nice to have someone to care about and who cares about me. I don't know what I'd do right now if I didn't have him to help me through things. It's nice to have one positive thing in my life.

Everything else seems to be falling apart. The tennis team, the play, my grades, my dream of being an engineer, my friendships—even my relationship with Mom and Dad has become strained now. Brad was right; because I'm so bad, everyone and everything seems to be rejecting me.

Brad. He's so great. I wonder why I feel sad when I have a wonderful guy. How can I feel happy and empty at the same time?

Someone bumped into her, causing her to stumble.

"Whoops, excuse me. Oh, hi, Elizabeth. How's it going?" It was Abby Parson, a girl from her history class.

"Hey, Abby. Sorry, I didn't mean to be in the way. I'm just on my way to class." She started to walk away, but Abby stopped her.

"Elizabeth, were you in an accident? What happened to your face?"

"Oh, nothing. A minor incident in physics." She laughed, but it sounded forced even to her own ears.

"That's why I stay away from the sciences." After a brief pause, Abby said, "I heard that you're not on the tennis team anymore. Is it true?"

"Yeah."

"Oh. That's too bad. So, I've been meaning to ask you about ECHO, our environmental club. I thought you were going to join."

"I changed my mind. Too busy."

"Well, it's not too late. We always welcome new members. Would you like to come to our next meeting?"

Elizabeth remembered her promise to Brad. "I appreciate the offer, Abby, but I don't think so. Sorry." *This way, I'll have more time to hang out with Brad. It's so sweet that he wants to be with me so much.* Despite this thought, she felt a little pang of regret at turning Abby down.

"No problem. I just thought I'd check. Well, I've gotta go. See ya!" Abby hurried off down the hall, leaving her alone again.

As Elizabeth headed to class, she noticed another sign for the tennis team. This one announced a pep rally after school. The team would leave for the state tournament early the next morning, and they were going to receive a big send-off. Elizabeth thought that she might go, just to cheer on her former teammates.

However, when the school day ended, she could not bring herself to go. She didn't know if she could bear the sight of Coach Thompson and the players all fired up to go to state. Besides, she wouldn't have anyone to sit with at the pep rally because Brad was at football practice. So, as many students filed into the gym to cheer for the tennis players, Elizabeth turned the other way and left the school.

She went home to wait for Brad's call.

CHAPTER 16

"**E**lizabeth, could you come in here, please?" As soon as Elizabeth shut the front door, she heard her mother calling from the living room.

"Sure, Mom. I'll be right there." Dropping her backpack in the entryway, she paused briefly to glance in the mirror centered above the hall table. She studied her reflection. Her summer tan had faded and she looked pale. Her straight hair hung limply near her shoulders. It, too, seemed to have lost its summer glow. The bruise on her cheek looked ugly. She brushed her hair forward with her fingers to try to cover it, but it didn't work. It only seemed to accentuate the frown on her face. Her whole body seemed to have lost its bounce. *I look awful. I'm lucky Brad is willing to stay with me.* With a sigh, she walked down the hallway, turned right, and took the two steps down into the sunken living room. Her mother was waiting on the sofa.

"Sit down, Elizabeth." She pointed to an overstuffed chair. "That bruise on your face still looks nasty. That must have been some physics experiment."

"It was. The smoke still hasn't cleared from the lab." A small smile appeared on Elizabeth's face but quickly disappeared. She found it hard to make jokes about what had happened. She didn't want to say too much because she was afraid her mother would sense that she was lying. She did not want her parents, or anyone, to discover the truth about what had happened. She could not let anyone know that Brad had hit her.

"Well, does that bad experiment have anything to do with this?" Her mother leaned forward and handed her a folded piece of paper. It was a progress report from her physics teacher informing her parents that she was currently earning a D- in class and that report cards were coming out very soon. The D- would likely be her quarter grade. "It came in the mail today," she said, her voice quiet but stern.

Elizabeth stared down at the paper and said nothing.

"Well, Elizabeth? Could you please explain this?"

She remained silent for several moments. When she finally spoke, she gave an answer that she thought her mother would accept. "I guess I have to learn better study habits now that I'm so busy. The varsity tennis team really takes up a lot of my time, and now the play does, too. I've got to budget my time better so I can excel at more than one thing at a time. I'm very sorry about the low grade, but I'm already working to raise it."

Elizabeth's mother crossed her legs and folded her hands across her knee. Inwardly, Elizabeth cringed. She knew that pose well—it meant that her mother was very upset. It didn't look like she bought her explanation. She braced herself.

"I'd like to believe that, Elizabeth. I truly would. And that little tale might actually have worked if I hadn't called the school this afternoon."

Elizabeth tensed. "What do you mean?"

"I called the guidance office after I read your progress report. Naturally, I assumed that there had been some mistake. Mr. Campbell, one of the counselors, did some checking for me. I was very surprised to discover when he called me back that the letter was indeed accurate. In addition to that, I discovered some additional tidbits about you, Elizabeth. When I asked Mr. Campbell if perhaps the tennis team, the play, and all those hard classes were too much for you to handle all at once, he informed me that you are no longer a member of the tennis team. It seems that you quit a while ago. Not only that, but you are no longer in the play; they removed you from the cast. Mr. Campbell also did some checking with your other teachers, and it turns out that you are doing poorly in all of your classes. What is going on, Elizabeth?"

Elizabeth could feel that her face was red, and her hands were trembling. She was terrified, sad, and angry all at once, and all of those emotions seemed to churn around in her stomach. She was terrified of what her mother's—and her father's—reaction might be. What would they do to her? Would they force her to break up with Brad? She was furious and defensive at the mere thought of that, but she was also very sad. She had disappointed her parents and herself. She had failed at all of the things that were once important to her. That thought also made her angry. Some of her priorities had changed, but her parents had no right to criticize her for making different choices than she had in the past. And to call the school! That thought prompted her to speak.

"The only thing that is 'going on,' Mother, is that I have changed my mind about what I like."

"Oh, really? Please explain. I'd love to hear it." Her tone could have made a snowman shiver.

"For one thing, I'm tired of tennis. I've been playing for years, and I'm sick of it. I didn't want to deal with the hassle anymore. And I discovered that I hate to act. I tried out; it didn't work. Big deal. Since when did you want me to become an actress, anyway?" Her mother opened her mouth to respond, but Elizabeth rushed on, afraid to lose momentum. "And so my grades have dropped. I don't like these subjects. When I get into classes I like, I'll get better grades."

"Well, this is all certainly news to me. The last I looked, my daughter loved to play tennis, loved to try new things and stick with them, and wanted very badly to become an engineer. When did you decide all this? And what about all of your tennis stuff that you took off the walls of your room? What's going on with you, Elizabeth?"

She shrugged. "Nothing. But why even ask me? Why don't you just call the school again? What a great way to spy on me to get juicy information."

"Cool it, Elizabeth. You will not address me in that tone. Since my conversation with Mr. Campbell, I've been doing some thinking, and I realized that these changes have come about since you started dating that Brad. Tonight I want you to talk to your father and me about your relationship with him. If I were you, I wouldn't make plans to see him anytime soon."

Elizabeth leaped up. "I knew it!" she shouted. "Brad was right! He knew that you'd try to keep us apart. He's just not good enough for you, is he? You can't tell me what to do! I'm not in grade school anymore, Mother. You couldn't keep me from quitting the tennis team, you couldn't force me to be in the play, you can't force me to keep taking classes I hate, and you can't keep me away from Brad!"

Elizabeth's mother remained seated and spoke calmly. "Elizabeth, please sit down. We cannot discuss this while you are throwing a tantrum."

"Babies throw tantrums, Mother! In case you haven't noticed, I'm not a baby anymore. I will not let you treat me like one!" With that, she turned and ran out of the living room, down the hallway, and out the front door. She slammed the door and ran down the sidewalk.

Elizabeth kept up her pace. She hadn't worked out since she left the tennis team and found that she was already a little out of shape, but she pushed herself forward. Her lungs burned, her sides ached, and her legs felt as though they were on fire, but she loved it. She had known that she missed tennis and working out, but she hadn't realized just how much. Running helped clear her mind. She was still very upset about her conversation with her mother, but she felt more focused now. The fear, the sadness, and the anger were all still there, but they were tamer inside her.

Before she realized it, she had run several miles and found herself on Brad's street. She knew where he lived, but she had never been inside his house before; he'd never invited her over. She noticed lights on inside. Excited to see him, she ran up his sidewalk and rang the doorbell.

The door opened after about a minute, and Brad stood in the entryway with a deep scowl on his face. "What are you doing here?"

"Well, it's good to see you, too," she breathed, slightly out of breath from her run.

"You didn't answer me."

"Oh, Brad, I just had to see you. I—"

"Now is not a good time, Elizabeth. I'm not in the mood. I haven't been home from football practice that long. My mother isn't here, so I'm trying to make supper.

What a pain. And I just got off the phone with my dad. Big surprise, I can't see him this weekend because he and my brother are going somewhere. So I think you'd better just go away."

"I can't. I don't know where to go. I don't want to go home because I just had a huge fight with my mother. My physics teacher sent her a letter telling her that I'm getting a D-, and she called the school to find out about it. She also found out about the tennis team and the play. She freaked out. She's really, really angry, and she doesn't want me to see you anymore. I don't want that to happen, Brad!" By now she had cooled down from her run, but she still had trouble breathing because she was on the verge of tears.

Brad stepped outside at once. "Oh, no, Liz! That sucks. Come on, let's go for a drive. I haven't started supper, anyway." He put his arm around her and led her to his car. "I'm glad you came to me, but you should have called me first. I would have met you somewhere. I don't want you coming to my house. Don't ever do that again," he said sternly.

"Why?"

He sat down in his car and slammed the door. Once Elizabeth was inside, he stared at her. "Why?" He raised his voice. "Why? Look at my house, Elizabeth. It's a dump, and I don't want you to see it, okay? It's pathetic."

"Brad, I don't think it's pathetic. I'm not—"

"Just drop it, Elizabeth." He fell silent as he drove down the street.

She sat quietly in the passenger seat, and the chance to slump down and brood over the entire day got the best of her. She started to cry. First, the tears streamed silently down her cheeks, and then she put her hands over her face and started to sob.

"Oh, Elizabeth, I'm sorry! I didn't mean to get so mad. I forget that you just do things without thinking. Even though you can be dumb, you sure are cute sometimes." He reached over and gave her arm a squeeze. She grabbed his hand and held onto it.

"Thanks, Brad. I'm glad you're so understanding. Today has been absolutely horrible!"

"Hey, I have an idea. There's a park and it's usually empty; why don't we go there and talk about it?"

She wiped her eyes and smiled at him. "That sounds nice. I'm glad I can always count on you no matter how horrible things are."

Brad parked the car and they got out. They walked silently toward the playground, holding hands, and Brad led Elizabeth to the swings where they each chose one and sat down. Elizabeth kept her feet on the ground, gently sliding them through the gravel and causing the swing to sway and twist slightly. Brad pumped his legs and was soon high up in the air. He laughed as he swished past Elizabeth. After awhile, he came to a stop. "Oh, yeah! That was fun! Now let's hear about this bad day."

She sighed. "I feel terrible, Brad. It started when I saw the signs for the tennis team all over the school, and it made me realize that I really miss it. I wish I wouldn't have quit."

"Really?" he said flatly. "I didn't realize you were so upset about being able to spend more time with me."

"No, that's not it at all."

"Then what is it? You just said you miss something that took you away from me. That's real nice."

"No, I don't mean it that way. And maybe I really don't miss it that much after all. Maybe I just feel bad because so many other bad things happened today. I know I failed my trig test, and that will bring my grade down. I'm doing poorly in every subject."

"Well, that's no surprise. You have to be smart to pass those classes."

"I can't believe you keep saying that. Maybe I'm not a genius, but I'm not stupid, you know."

"Don't argue with me, Elizabeth. You can't be that intelligent or you'd be doing better in school."

"I don't think that's it."

"What, then?" His tone was harsh, and Elizabeth said nothing. He jumped off his swing and paced in front of her. "Are you blaming me?"

"Well, no, but—"

"I can't believe you!" he roared. "You think it's my fault that you're a moron?"

She looked at the ground, unsure of what to say.

"Get off that stupid swing, Elizabeth." He lurched forward and, slamming both hands against her shoulders, shoved her backward. She tumbled off, and her head hit the ground with a loud thud.

She staggered to her feet. "That hurt! What did you do that for?"

"Now I guess you're going to blame me for something else."

"No, I'm not!" She was close to tears again, but she did not want to cry in front of him right now. "Look, just forget everything, okay? I had a bad day and I just wanted to talk to you about it. I wasn't trying to blame you for anything."

"Well, it seems to me like you're accusing me of ruining your life." He began to mock her. "'My life is so miserable. I wish I was on the tennis team. I wish I could spend all of my time studying for no reason. I wish I didn't have to spend any time at all with my stupid boyfriend.'" His face was red, and he moved toward her. "Thanks a lot, Elizabeth. I try to make it so we can be together, but you just think I'm a loser."

As he said the last word, he used both hands to shove Elizabeth again. She stumbled but caught her balance. This seemed to enrage him further, and he hit her hard across the face. This time she fell into the gravel. "Stand up, Elizabeth," he roared as he grabbed her by the arm and yanked her to her feet.

"Brad, let go! That really hurts!" But he didn't let go. He gripped her arm even tighter and twisted it hard. Elizabeth cried out in pain.

"There. That'll make it so you can't play tennis, you ungrateful cow!" With another yank he released her arm and gave her a hard push that propelled her forward.

She crashed headfirst into the swing set's metal pole and fell onto the ground in a heap. Too dizzy and sore to move, she held still. She heard him crunch on the gravel and saw his feet inches from her face. The noise stopped, but only for a moment. His shoe slid quickly and heavily across the gravel, and flying rocks bombarded her face. The tiny rocks stung her cheeks, and she choked when they invaded her mouth. They hit her eyes, and a scratching, burning pain shot through her head. With the rocks came Brad's foot; it slammed into her side. Elizabeth heard a sickening crack as more intense pain flashed through her body. Thankfully, she didn't feel the pain for long. Darkness overcame her, and she lost consciousness. She didn't see Brad flee, and she didn't know that she lay on the ground for nearly fifteen minutes before two joggers noticed her and called an ambulance.

CHAPTER 17

Elizabeth stretched out on the couch in the same room in which she and her mother had argued only a few days before. Today was Sunday, and she sat wrapped in a soft blanket with her legs outstretched. She leaned against the mass of pillows her mother had arranged for her and closed her eyes, willing the painkillers to kick in. Her head throbbed, her face hurt, her arm, nestled in its sling, was in pain, and it was excruciating to take a deep breath. Thankfully, she had no long-term injuries; in fact, the hospital had released her late yesterday afternoon. She was glad to be home.

Neither of her parents had mentioned the fight that she had with her mother. They also didn't mention the fact that Elizabeth had stormed out of the house without permission. They showed only concern toward Elizabeth and anger toward Brad.

She opened her eyes when she heard the doorbell ring. She could hear voices down the hallway; it was her mother, and she thought that one of the other voices belonged to Meg. Someone else was there, too, but she couldn't tell who it was. She was curious why Meg was there, and wondered who had come with her, but she was too sore to wander down the hall to check it out. She figured that eventually her mom would direct Meg and the other person to the living room, so she just sat and waited. This time, she was not upset at the thought of seeing Meg. She was a little nervous, since she had been so nasty to her the last time they were together, but she also realized that she was excited to see her. Despite what she had been telling herself about growing apart from Meg, she had really missed her and wanted to revive their friendship.

———

Down the hall, Elizabeth's mother had greeted Meg with a hug. "Meg, dear, thank you for coming. I hope you don't mind that I called you."

"Absolutely not, Mrs. Carter. I'm so glad you did. I brought someone along; this is Sarah Wilson." She introduced Elizabeth's mom to Brad's old girlfriend.

"It's nice to meet you, Sarah."

"Thanks. I'm glad to have the chance to meet you, too. Meg brought me along for a reason. I used to date Brad, and he abused me, too. Now it seems like I was lucky; he did hit me sometimes, but I never wound up in the hospital."

"Oh, you poor thing. I'm glad you weren't hospitalized, but it doesn't make you lucky."

"I know, but..." She trailed off. "How's Elizabeth doing?"

"She's sore. Come on, let's go see her." Mrs. Carter led the girls down the hall. Before taking them into the living room, she stopped and peered around the corner. "Elizabeth? You have company. Can we come in?" When

Elizabeth nodded, she came down the two steps with Meg and Sarah in tow.

Meg gasped, and tears sprung to her eyes. "Oh, Elizabeth! You look terrible! I'm so sorry this happened. Are you okay?"

"Yes, I am. I feel pretty bad now, but I'm actually glad that it happened." She noticed Sarah standing off to the side. "Hi, Sarah. Thanks for coming. Why don't all of you sit down? You're making me feel lazy; I don't want to be the only one on a couch!"

Her little joke seemed to relax everyone somewhat. Meg, Sarah, and her mom all sat down, but no one spoke for a while. Finally, Elizabeth broke the silence.

"I owe all of you an apology. I have been just awful to everyone, and I'm very sorry. I guess I really haven't been myself lately."

Sarah spoke next. "How could you be yourself? You were being controlled by that jerk."

"True," she admitted, "but you tried to warn me early in the school year. I guess I didn't want to listen. I really didn't believe you. Meg, I'm sorry I got so mad when you tried to warn me, too. I honestly believed that Brad and I were in love and that everyone was jealous of what we had. Boy was I wrong!"

"Don't be too hard on yourself," Sarah said. "That's the thing about Brad and people like him. They can be very sweet and can do a very good job of convincing you that your relationship is based on love. And I'm sure Brad really does care about you, Elizabeth. If he didn't, he wouldn't work so hard to control you, and he wouldn't get so mad every time he thinks he's losing control."

"That does not excuse any of his behavior," Mrs. Carter said crisply.

"I agree," Meg chimed in. "I think Brad was horrible from the very beginning, and I don't think his behavior was in any way loving."

"It is twisted," agreed Sarah. "That's one of the most dangerous things about the whole thing: emotionally abusive people are sneaky, and they can make you think that they are very loving and caring. They work it so you think you have the problem and are just lucky to have them. I know—I was involved with Brad for two years, remember?"

"That's why I'm glad this happened," Elizabeth said quietly. "It really opened my eyes. I'm afraid I might have continued to date Brad and let him control me otherwise. Look at what he did in such a short time: He made me quit the tennis team; I was kicked out of the play because of him; my grades have dropped because I spent every night on the phone with him rather than studying, and he convinced me that I was too stupid for those classes. He even sabotaged my relationships with the people I care most about.

"But despite those things, he was also very sweet to me. He always wanted to be with me or talk to me. That made me feel loved. I just didn't realize he was making me give up my relationships and activities, but he wasn't giving up anything.

"Also, Brad did make me feel wanted. He's going through some awful things at home; he kept telling me that he needed me, and I bought it. I hate to admit it, since now it seems so ridiculous, but I wouldn't have seen the true Brad if he hadn't beaten me up.

"Now, though, there's no way I'll go back to him. I haven't talked to him yet, but when I do, it will be for the last time. Our relationship is over."

"Yay!" exclaimed Meg.

Elizabeth looked at her. "See? I told you you were jealous."

"No, Lizzie, I swear I'm not. That's not what I meant. I don't—" Meg was talking rapidly, but Elizabeth managed to cut her off anyway.

"Meg, I'm kidding."

"Lizzie, that was mean! I'd throw a pillow at you if you didn't look so pathetic right now."

"Elizabeth, I'm very proud of you, and I'm glad to hear you say that you are through with Brad." Her mother paused and then continued, "However, I'm afraid that breaking up with Brad might not be as easy as you think."

"She's right," Sarah responded. "I wanted to get rid of Brad long before we actually broke up, but it was extremely difficult."

"What happened?" asked Elizabeth.

"I'd be happy to tell you everything, but let's concentrate on you first. Did you press charges against him for assault?"

"No, I didn't. The police talked to me, and I told them the truth, but even though I'm through with Brad, I just couldn't press charges. He does have some problems in his life, and I don't want to add to them. Plus, it wouldn't change what happened to me. If anything, I thought it might make things more difficult if I run into him at school." Elizabeth glanced at her mother and saw the look on her face. She quickly added, "Mom and Dad want me to press charges, though. The police officer said I have some time to decide. I can't wait too long, but I can think about it for a while. I'll see how things go, I guess."

Sarah sat thoughtfully for a moment, and then responded, "I can see your point about not wanting to press charges. I do think you should consider it, though.

He needs to face the consequences for what he did to you, and it might actually be pretty powerful help in keeping him away from you. At least think about it. It's a good thing you told the police exactly what happened; it could help you in the future. You might need to get a restraining order against him. He probably won't just let you go. I had some counseling when I was trying to break up with Brad, and that was part of the advice I received. My parents and I ended up going away to visit relatives this summer, so I never did go that route, but it is a possibility you should consider."

"Wow," said Meg. "What a mess."

"I know," agreed Elizabeth. "I'm really sorry that this whole thing started in the first place, but I'm very glad it's ending. I know it might be rough, but it can't be worse than these past couple of months. I'll get through it."

"We're all here to help you, Lizzie," said Meg.

"That's right, but you can't shut us out anymore."

"I won't, Mom. That was partly Brad's doing, too."

"Partly?"

"Well, if I hadn't been dating him I never would have separated myself from my friends and family, but I am an independent person and I allowed myself to get pulled under Brad's influence."

"Elizabeth, do not blame yourself for any of this!" Sarah's response was passionate.

"Oh, I'm not. It's just that I let him take over. I was so happy to be dating the almighty Brad Evans that I took his crap. And I came to believe it. I actually believed that I was lucky that he would put up with me."

"That's what people like him do. They have a very sneaky way of taking you over. This is not your fault."

Just then the doorbell rang, and Mrs. Carter went to answer it. A few minutes later, she staggered back into the room under the weight of a life-size teddy bear and an enormous bouquet of flowers.

Meg jumped up to help her; she took the vase and carried it to the coffee table. She grabbed the card attached to the flowers and handed it to Elizabeth. Elizabeth opened the card, read it silently, and then handed it back to Meg, who read it and passed it around the room. It read , "You are worth more to me than I can buy with my dad's allowance. Please forgive me. I love you very much. Brad."

Elizabeth sighed. "It is going to be tough to get rid of him, isn't it?"

Sarah nodded slowly and replied, "Yes."

CHAPTER 18

Elizabeth walked into school on Tuesday and headed for her locker. She was still very sore and her headache had not disappeared, but she did not want to stay at home another day. For one thing, she was determined to bring up her grades, and to do that she had to go to class. For another, she wanted to confront Brad and officially end their relationship. She had absolutely no doubts about it, but she was extremely nervous nonetheless.

As she expected, Brad was standing by her locker. He rushed up to meet her. "Oh, Liz! How are you feeling? I've tried calling you, but no one ever answered. I guess you were resting. I can't believe I did this to you!" His eyes were watery, but Elizabeth ignored it and he kept talking. "Oh, I'm such a loser. I was feeling like crap the other day and I took it out on you. I was so wrong. I will never, ever act that way again. That's no way to treat the person I love. To seal my promise, I bought you this." He held out a little gold box and opened it for her. Inside was a gold ring with a small sparkling sapphire in the center. "I know how you love the color blue. This is a symbol of my love for you and my vow that I'll never harm you again."

She didn't take it. "Elizabeth?" he questioned.

Elizabeth thought that her stomach contained millions of butterflies—not mere Monarchs, but gigantic Queen Alexandra's Birdwings. Willing her voice to stay steady and not betray her anxiety, she replied, "That's nice of you, Brad, but I can't accept it. I know you won't harm me again because I'm ending our relationship. I will not see you anymore." She was pleased that her voice sounded clear and confident. Rehearsing this scene with Meg had paid off.

"No, Elizabeth! Please don't break up with me. I don't want to lose you! I love you. I need you." He tried to shove the ring into her hands.

She crossed her arms. Pain shot through her right arm, but she willed herself not to flinch. "I'm sorry, Brad. It's over. You may think you love me, but the way you act toward me is not the way to treat someone you love. And whether or not you love me, I do not love you. I thought I did, but I was wrong."

Brad jammed the ring into his pocket. He belted the locker beside him and shouted, "I can't believe it! I make one little mistake and this is how you act? You should think twice about what you're saying. Look at you—you're a loser! You have no friends, you're not involved in anything, you have no life. What will you do without me? You cannot end our relationship!" He hit the locker again.

Elizabeth noticed that people around them were staring, but didn't care. She needed to do this, no matter how uncomfortable or awful it was. "I will thrive again, Brad. That's what I will do without you." She stared at him as he seethed. His face was red and he was breathing rapidly, but he also looked panicked. His green eyes bored into hers and seemed to beg her to stay. He ran his hand through his black hair, tousling it and making him appear innocent.

Shaking her head, she said, "Sorry, Brad. You blew it. You've lost me."

She turned around quickly and headed down the hall. She knew that this would not be her last confrontation with Brad, but now that the first one was over, she felt that she could handle the others. She walked a few yards away to where Meg was waiting. Together, they joined the crowd of people in the hall and walked away.

Tanya J. Peterson currently lives on the west coast with her husband and two children. She is a teacher in a school for homeless and runaway adolescents. Previously, she has published a short story entitled "Challenge!" and a book review for <u>Counseling Today</u>. This is her first novel.

1361992R00089

Made in the USA
San Bernardino, CA
12 December 2012